Titan II: 54 Hidden Missiles!

By Dan Murray

Text copyright © 2023 Dan Murray

All Rights Reserved

Edited by Becky Gingras, D.P.A.

Front and back cover photos by United States Air Force (USAF), from Wikimedia (public domain).

This is a work of military fiction. Any similarity to any actual person, living or dead, is coincidental. Government and commercial products and programs are trademarked or copyrighted. To the best of the author's knowledge, there is no hidden weapons program as portrayed here. The Titan II, airport, and other systems' tech data are public information available from the internet and should not be relied upon for actual flight. This work is not an operator's manual. The latitudes and longitudes in this novel were obtained from the internet.

This adventure novel portrays many foibles from people in the 20th century, including dishonesty, violence, political crime, sexual activities, and vulgar language. If this isn't to your liking, the author recommends three of his personal favorites: *Time and Again*, by Jack Finney; *The Wind in the Willows*; and *Rabbit Hill*.

This novel is often set in a Titan II missile silo. The author and editor recommend going online and viewing a cut-away drawing of a Titan II silo complex, among other photos you may find interesting. Multiple websites may provide drawings and the Titan Missile Museum website (TitanMissileMuseum.org) may provide useful background info.

Table of Contents

Acknowledgements, Preface, Introduction

Chapter 1: An Unusual Job Offer..1

Chapter 2: At Home in Connecticut......................................23

Chapter 3: Rejuvenation..26

Chapter 4: Susan..40

Chapter 5: Sandy and Jeffrey..58

Chapter 6: Somebody's Watching..62

Chapter 7: An Unsettling Meeting..67

Chapter 8: Seduction in the Morgue....................................82

Chapter 9: The Combat Crew's Arrival.................................89

Chapter 10: Hidden No More..102

Chapter 11: The Shell Game...116

Chapter 12: Complications..135

Chapter 13: Sex and Paratroopers......................................149

Chapter 14: The Plane at the Bottom of the Lake................177

Chapter 15: Launch!..182

Chapter 16: The Quick and the Dead..................................190

Chapter 17: A Meeting With Amanda..................................197

Afterword..205

The Author and Production Team..206

Acknowledgements

The author would like to thank Becky Gingras, D.P.A. (California) for her assistance in editing this book. Thanks also to Joe Kruyla of The Shipping Grounds (Denville, New Jersey) for preparing the draft proof copies.

Special thanks to the families who let us use their pre- and post-rejuvenation photos. The new government rejuvenation process is an astounding success!

Preface

In September 2022, I read a research article about the success a research team has had in growing a mouse fetus not from a mom and dad, but from other cells. Included in the project was the start of growing the brain and heart. Eventually, we'll grow replacement human and pet body parts at organ farms. Or use 3D printers to print replacement organs such as livers. Give us 500 years and we'll be able to copy entire adult humans.

One can look back 500 years to 1700 and clearly see how far we've developed technically. But emotionally, we still function at about the year 1200. We feel jealousy, anger, bitterness, sympathy, empathy, love. Those emotions, unlike our technology, haven't changed.

That's enough to ponder for now, I suppose.

Enjoy the story.

Introduction

Oh brave new world, That has such people in't.

–The Tempest

Some 54 Titan II ICBM liquid-fueled missiles in Kansas, Arkansas, and Arizona were deactivated as obsolete by 1987. Another 54 were hidden in manned silos in Colorado, Utah, and Wyoming. Through a classified government program, those 54 obsolete liquid-fueled missiles, each with 10 upgraded 9-mt warheads, were still manned by civilians being paid one million dollars each. This took place long after the missiles were thought to have been removed.

This blockbuster military novel follows one of those crews in the path of an asteroid hurtling towards Earth at 85,000 mph.

Chapter 1: New York City

Robert Molini, retired Lt. Col., USAF, walked into the New York City office building at 1212 Avenue of the Americas and showed the guard the certified letter verifying his appointment to see retired Lieutenant General Douglas Birmingham, formerly the head of Strategic Air Command headquartered at Offutt Air Force Base, Nebraska. Robert remembered the general's name from active duty but had never met him. Taking the elevator to the fifth floor of the office building, Robert wondered what the general could possibly want with a longtime retired serviceman. The company headed by the general was called NASS, Inc., which stood for North American Security Services. Other than that, Robert had found little useful info from searching the internet for public records, which listed only two employees and a few thousand dollars of revenue a year. Clearly, if the general were involved, there was more to the picture. Subsidiary companies, phantom employees...Robert found the whole thing rather intriguing.

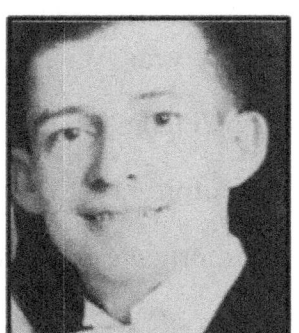

A photo of Robert taken during dinner at The Mayflower Hotel, Washington, D.C. (post-rejuvenation).

Robert knocked on the office door and entered. The anteroom was empty, with no secretary present. It was a sterile waiting room with undistinguished pictures, plastic chairs, and standard blue carpet with the USAF symbol woven into it. A sensor must have alerted the general that his guest had arrived, for within a minute, the general opened the door from his inner office and came out, hand extended.

"Robert, I remember you from your time as a Titan II alternate command post commander. You had a solid record."

"General, I seem to recall your name also. It's been a few years."

"That it has. Come inside. Our company doesn't put much into show and fancy offices, but we're thriving on government contracts and work. We're into some unusual efforts I thought you might like to be a part of."

"So this meeting is a job interview?"

"Oh, yes, and a most unusual job. Like nothing you ever dreamed of after retiring from service. Some of our government contracts are strictly black ops types of jobs, but not little jobs like undercover in a foreign country for a few weeks. We're into long-term operations – years, sometimes – with world-wide ramifications. In fact, part of our spending is straight from the Secretary of Defense's classified budget, and we're talking millions every year. Want some coffee?"

"No, thanks, general. I had lunch up the street on the way in."

"You're living up in Stamford now?"

"Yes. Cape Cod house, mortgage, kids in high school, that sort of thing."

"Wife?"

Robert shrugged rather than say anything bad about her.

"You know how it gets to be, general."

"That we do. We do, indeed." He looked at Robert and Robert looked back.

"I have a proposition for you – a job, if you will – that pays very, very well with a huge bonus in five years if you stay in the position. You're uniquely qualified, too."

"Yes, sir?"

"What I'm about to offer you is Top Secret, strictly between the two of us. It would be catastrophic to national security if word of what I'm going to offer you were to reach the public sector. Is that clear?"

"Yes, sir. Very clear."

"The company I work for, NASS, is employed by the Air Force and the DoD to hire people with certain qualifications to return to doing what they did while on active duty, or be trained to do so. NASS concentrates on USAF programs. Other companies deal with Navy, Army, Coast Guard, and Marine programs. I help manage one program only. Other NASS managers deal with other USAF programs. NASS is a black ops company, meaning we are secretly funded under American black ops programs. Even Congress doesn't know what we do. Certainly the president and Cabinet don't know, nor the USAF Chief of Staff. The program is well-buried and well-funded, mostly being run by retired generals. We do have contact, of course, with the Pentagon's budget offices and the National Command Authority, but not at the very top. This ensures if anything should ever go public, any knowledge of it can be denied. Can't have the president knowing something that may embarrass the country."

"Of course not," Robert replied.

The general paused a minute before getting to the point.

"Robert, we know you are in deep financial trouble, your marriage is worthless, you don't love your wife and she doesn't love you, you're not close to your kids, you're seeing a psychiatrist for depression, and in general, based on emails to your old college friends, you would do anything to turn back the clock to when you were 19 and engaged again to the woman who ended up marrying someone else. I understand the two of you were engaged for four years. You threw that away by doing the noble thing, and you wouldn't get involved in drugs since you'd planned a future in the USAF. True?"

Robert sat still for a minute before replying.

"Yes, sir. There's no point in denying anything since you seem to know everything already."

"You tried to be an effective officer and you had a good record, but promotions to high rank didn't happen because you weren't married to the right sort of spouse. She never supported, much less participated in military life, and you paid the price for that. Spouses are important to promotions for high rank, and yours didn't do you any favors by saying negative things about military life. She wasn't the sort of woman to help you get promoted. Otherwise, your retired pay might be more and your life less a struggle. But this job could change all that. Tell me, how would you like to be as happy as you were back when you planned to marry Susan?"

"That's difficult to achieve now, isn't it, general?"

"Nothing is impossible with NASS at your side. That's our slogan, though we don't publicize it much."

"What, exactly, is the offer?"

"It's rather simple. You go back to the Titan II weapon system, underground, in a highly isolated area. You get medical coverage for you and your family, contributions into a retirement plan, a tax-free salary, and a one-million-dollar tax-free bonus at the end of five years. If you're happy, you can stay in the position for as long as your health allows it, and every five years you receive another million-dollar bonus, plus annual salary increases every year after five years. We have some people who've been working for us now for many years and they quite enjoy it."

Robert listened carefully, then gathered his thoughts before speaking.

"You said Titan II. That system was deactivated from combat alert status. Only the space launch program using Titan boosters is still active, and that program is about to end when it runs out of launch vehicles."

The general stared intently at Robert before continuing.

"Robert, this is very classified, so much so that this office – bland and ordinary as it might appear – is really a bug-free lead capsule. No technology can eavesdrop on what we're saying in here. The Titan program and many other DoD programs that the public and our enemies think were deactivated, were not. They still exist, and are often manned by retired veterans such as yourself. This includes an extensive number of programs. Ever wondered if all those WWII diesel subs were really scrapped? I can tell you they were mothballed on the bottom of Chesapeake Bay, not far from Norfolk Naval Base. All these countries – China, India, North Korea – boasting about how their diesel subs can sneak up on our carriers and sink them…They haven't a clue we've got 400 diesel subs ready to go to war that no one knows about. We don't have full crews for all 400, of course, but we have maintenance crews on each sub4. They could train new crew members in three months to start doing war patrols against foreign diesel subs, if needed. We never scrapped them at the end of WWII – we just hid them. They have live torpedoes, too."

"And Titan II?"

"The alert silos at Little Rock, Wichita, and Tucson that the public knew about were deactivated. But a duplicate set of 54 silos was built in the late 1960s in the Wyoming, Utah and Colorado mountains. They're on government land far away from civilization, fenced off and well patrolled. The program was justified as training silos. Then people retired, the land was cordoned off, and people forgot about the silos. As

I said, the area is well patrolled. Airspace is controlled, too, but with good camouflage, nothing can be seen from the air."

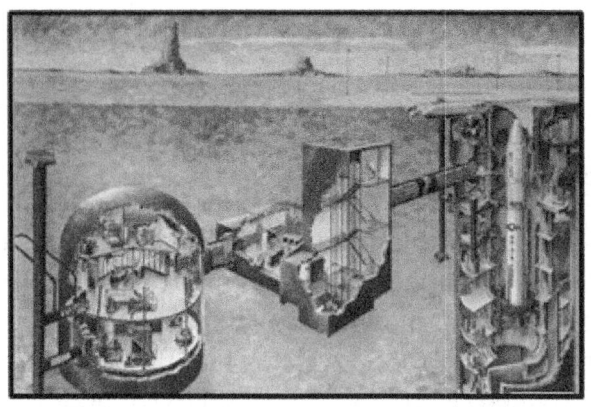

Titan II complex, original design. Entrance and elevator center. Missile on right. Control Center and living areas on left. DoD. (Public domain.)

"What about infrared imaging and satellites?"

"Some of the waste heat is piped miles away. What do you think makes hot springs in the area? Waste heat is expelled at the bottom of man-made lakes or even into natural streams if it's not hot enough to kill the fish. In fact, in Colorado, the trout thrive on a warmer stream. They grow all year and get to be a pretty good size. Some expelled heat is vented close by, and we hope it isn't noticed. It's not roaring hot like a rocket exhaust."

"Do I get to go fishing?"

The general chuckled. "No, sorry. There's no leaving the silo. Or even going up top. We can't have prying eyes or satellites identifying patterns of people moving around. In the silo you stay. We're considering allowing two crew topside at night, though. By the time you get on crew, we may have liberalized that rule."

"And this is for five years?"

"Yes. And for a million-dollar bonus. And you'll have cameras and microphones so you can keep up with what's happening in the world. TV, cable, internet, all the modern gadgets and video games."

"In the old days we were on a crew. Are there three others?"

"Of course. One is a retired facilities technician for the air conditioning and so forth. You remember."

"We called them MFTs. Maintenance Facility Technicians. They could fix almost anything. We gave them the nickname 'Mighty Fine Technicians.' They were good troops, and lots of 'em were staff sergeants."

"You're getting a retired master sergeant. Last assignment was as a technical facilities instructor at Wichita Falls, Texas, at the air base there."

"And the other crew members?"

"A reserve sergeant and a reserve officer. You'll all be together for five years, unless someone quits. We've trained the reserve tech sergeant. She's your ballistic missile analyst technician – BMAT."

"A person can quit?"

"Of course, but no bonus, and the salary and health care stop. And you go back to your former life of being unhappy."

Robert smiled wryly. "You seem very sure people will like being underground for five years."

"We are. We've had less than a 3% loss from people quitting. We've lost a few to accidents and some to mental and physical illness, but the loss rate is well under 10%. The mental challenge can be difficult, but most people adapt well since they were in ICBMs on active duty."

"There's more about the crew?" Robert asked.

The general paused for effect.

"There is, but maybe you have other questions or concerns?"

"Those five years. That's like being in isolation. No one to be close to for all that time? At least now I have a wife, even if we aren't very close emotionally. She's at least there *physically*."

The general lit a cigar and took a few puffs, put his elbows on the desk, and stared at Robert. "You don't think we've thought this all through? We have some very smart people working on this project. We've spent years achieving our goal of a multi-layered defense posture. You're not the first person we've hired. There are hundreds of your type underground right now, very happy to be in a launch silo for five years."

"If you have all these people, why hire me?"

"We had a recent casualty. A very odd one. Electrocuted. He was wearing a ring when he shouldn't have been. He got careless and got electrocuted. We're still not exactly sure why. He was alone with one of our RNs before the rest of the crew arrived, doing a blood pressure check. With 480 volts down there, we strictly prohibit people wearing rings. He was wearing one and obviously shouldn't have been. Got himself electrocuted, so we have a vacancy. We're doing some shuffling and you'll be commanding a new crew."

Robert nodded, his eyes focused on the general's body language. "You never told me why people don't quit."

The general took another puff of his cigar. "They don't quit because they're happy down there."

"And why, exactly, are they so happy, General? What's the key to happiness for people living in an old silo?"

"It's actually very simple. NASS gives them back the love of their life. The person they lost when they were young. Those other two crew members are female. We'll have one paired with you and one with the sergeant. And neither will be strangers. You know the young lady you'll be with. The same holds true for the sergeant."

Robert looked at the general with confusion. "I'm sorry, sir. I'm afraid I don't understand. You said I know her?"

"You most certainly do. You know each other very well. *Intimately*, in fact. How would you like to have her back in your life for five years?"

With that, the general opened a white envelope and pushed a photo across the desk to Robert.

"That was taken last week," the general said as Robert stared at the photo in disbelief.

"No. It can't be. You never met her. She left me just before I entered the Air Force. Ended up marrying the son of some wealthy entrepreneur. I married someone else, too – the day before I entered active duty. I always wanted a big family, and she was okay with that."

"It's *Susan*, Robert. It really is her. She's waiting for you if you want the job. Everything you remember will be the same. We can turn back the clock and make memories come alive. She's yours, willingly. All yours. As if you were 19 again. Both of you."

"How can that be?" he asked, unable to look away from the black and white photo of her in a dark bikini. He knew without asking it was purple, her favorite color.

The general puffed on his cigar again. "You remember when you had your appendix removed last year?"

"Yes. It happened so suddenly."

"It would seem that way. The liver trouble you had which put you in the hospital was caused by our misuse of a drug named Augmentin.

The downstream effect was a bad appendix. Sort of another little side effect from us." The general chuckled.

"How would you know that? The doctors never found a cause, and I got better after they removed my appendix. The liver trouble vanished."

"I know because we gave Augmentin to you instead of the flu shot you thought you were getting at the flu clinic offered by your employer. When you went through the line, another syringe was used by a nurse working for us. You got a large dose – a *very* large dose – which caused problems with your liver. In the hospital, we gave you a sleeping injection on top of your regular dose of Mirtazapine. We have lots of nurses working for us across the country. Hundreds of them. Then we wheeled in a very special video machine, put a band around your head, and recorded what you dreamed. A few whispered words encouraged certain dreams. We recorded the visual images."

"No one can do that," Robert said, his voice little more than a whisper. "It's not possible. Making a video of dreams…They tried it with dogs under a classified DAPA project."

"Not marketed, you mean. The Defense Advanced Projects Agency has been doing stuff like this for years. We *can* do it, and we do it on prospective employees so we can give them happiness if they come work for us. We know exactly what you dream about Susan when you dream of her. I'm sure you don't want to see the recordings. Their explicit nature would be rather shocking to those not used to seeing such things. They are safely coded and locked away underground in Maryland, near the National Military Alternate Command Center. There's no direct identification to you."

Robert shook his head. "You can't have gotten her to agree to live with me for five years."

"Of course we did. And she's 19 again. Wearing purple for you. Remember, that photo you're looking at was taken last week."

"She'd be past middle age."

"Not now. Now she's 19. And so will you, after we do a few things."

"You mean like surgery?"

"Some, but not very much. More like genetic coding rearrangement. We can turn your genetic code back in time. Redesign your makeup, basically. We put your blood through a certain machine, the molecules in your blood go back into you changed, and that blood changes all of you. You'll be unconscious. We've discovered that a person's brain has trouble adjusting to loss of certain recent memories if they're awake. It induces psychosis, and we can't have that if you're going back into nuclear weapons. You have to be stable, not out of your mind."

Robert stood up, his face red. "Wait, general. What the fuck? Those 54 old, fatigued missiles you mentioned, most of which are probably leaking – you're telling me they're nuclear armed? They were built years ago. Like two generations ago. You're telling me they've got live warheads on them? A 9 mt was the largest ever deployed."

"Robert, sit down and listen. This is the greatest defense project we've ever pulled off. And remember, it isn't just Titan that's been resurrected. The Navy and Army have similar programs, too. All classified, of course."

A crew on Level 2, Control Center, working through the launch checklist. DoD. (Public domain.)

Robert sat, his heart racing.

"Yes, those missiles are armed. That's the whole point. What do you think, Robert? Why else would we save an obsolete weapon system that cost billions of dollars? We don't care about historic value. Henry Ford said history is bunk, and he was right. Our goal is to blow somebody's ass off if our enemies give us any grief. Those 54 missiles are live. Fueled, armed, 9 mt warhead. Ready to fly off to China, Pakistan, or wherever. They can reach more than 8,700 miles. In the SALT talks, we lied about the number of warheads the US had manufactured over the years. We played the shell game. The president back then went along with the lie but thought the warheads were stored as a reserve force. He never knew they were on the missiles, ready to go. We can drop a big hammer on any nation around the world within 35 minutes. We can blow 'em straight to hell. If some leader disrespects us, we can take 'em out in 30 minutes. In support of our Titan project, we're forming a new crew with you as the commander."

"You're telling me you want to hire me to go back on active alert status with a nuclear armed missile down the hallway, a hodgepodge, ragtag crew of greenies who've never trained together, including two women who want to screw with us, and all of us will look and feel as if we're 19 again? This is absolute, total lunacy. What about a 19-year-old's emotions? What about the technical system knowledge we need? If the fuel and oxidizer meet, they burn with no ignition system required. They're poisonous as hell, too, and there have been deaths. Being liquid fueled and prone to accidents was one of the reasons why the missiles were deactivated in the first place."

He continued as the general nodded. "One error and the whole silo could explode. That's what happened at Little Rock. That didn't just happen out of the blue. Someone in maintenance dropped a wrench down beside the missile, which put a hole in the side of it. It started leaking and eventually exploded. I saw the after-event photos. The silo and all three levels of the control center were demolished. *Gone.* The explosion turned that concrete silo to dust. General, that fuel and oxidizer are incredibly dangerous. And you're going to put people down there who feel like they're 19? What if they're facing the crisis of their young lives? And you're doing this with people who've never worked together, and whose brains have been altered? It takes time for four people to become a functional unit. That's what training is for: to prevent mistakes. I haven't been on alert for years. How finely tuned do you think I am after spending years on the couch watching television? I haven't been a crew commander in years."

Robert went on. "A long time ago, I went TDY to a military school in Alabama. When I came back to the wing after 90 days, I didn't get my wing instructor position back right away. I needed retooling. I was forgetful and slow. I was retrained, had a bunch of simulator rides, and was assigned as a regular line crew commander. I was terrified. I had two one-stripers coming in from tech and ops schools, plus 45 days wing training, and a newly promoted 1Lt. I was the only one with a high number of alerts. My clothes were worn and faded, and I looked scruffy and exhausted. I looked miserable – and I *was* back then.

"Even though I was exhausted, I still slept like a cat. The slightest variation in noise down there, and I was out of my rack and on my feet, running down the stairs before the alarms even sounded. My crew bag was all banged up from being thrown into a Huey for silo transport. The new guys always looked nice in their pressed blues, new boots, and new patches. Those guys didn't know shit about the real world down there, and all the ways you could die. Fuel, oxidizer, 480 volts, sidearm accident, helicopter accident, high pressure line break, falls, rattlesnakes on the entrance steps, motor vehicle accidents from lack of sleep…They didn't know shit.

"There were plenty of times when I was up all night. I might've been teaching FNGs all night because maintenance was there all day, or a team was doing night repairs, or there was a thunderstorm, or battle exercises…whatever. I remember one time we had safety violations and for a while, they made it where only crew commanders could refuel vehicles and drive. So someone who'd been awake all night had to drive 50 miles back to base with the other crew members, and they were probably so tired that everything was a blur.

"People got ulcers all the time. I had one during my final year down there. That's the nature of it all. You're putting people unprepared for that level of stress into a situation involving nuclear weapons. Talk about being stressed-out and on-edge. I bet you've never pulled alerts down there. Missile duty isn't like aircraft alert. From your high-ranking position, sir, you can't see all the shit that people on missile alert deal with every day, where one mistake could kill everyone."

The general sighed in dismay. "Robert, are you finished with all this? Anything else you feel compelled to tell me?"

"Oh yes, General. There's lots more. I've spent a lot of time down there. Maybe you'll come to see the real situation with making people 19 again, and how this program is headed for a wreck someday. I hope you have security personnel with these silos who know what they're doing, because I saw a lot in my time who didn't. The security teams of two Air Police ate and bunked in crew quarters with us. They could stay at any one of the silos they patrolled for 24 hrs. For some reason, those fuckers could barely get through the day without getting lost or getting their vehicle stuck in mud or snow, or driving into a ditch. There was a rule that their M16s had to be unloaded topside before they came underground. It didn't matter, though. These assholes would come strolling into the control center with the full mags still in their M16s. We're damn lucky someone in the control center didn't get his ass shot off. The APs could be told 20 times that security personnel can't bring loaded M16s underground, and they still did. One guy cleaning his revolver one night screwed up and put a bullet through the commander's launch console because he didn't unload the weapon before cleaning it. The bullet went through the fire emergency spray button. Left a big-ass hole and sprayed the missile with 10,000 gallons of water. Completely destroyed the on-board electronics.

"Or how about when the security teams got onto the silo door, played burlesque music from a tape recorder, turned on their Jeeps' headlights, and danced in a chorus line, kicking their boots in the air? Some of them tried playing a recording of march music. They marched around on top of the silo door, twirled their M16s like batons, and some dumbass shot himself in the leg. So we lost sleep waiting for the medevac helo to fly out from the base and take them to the hospital. Then, when we got back, we lost more sleep filling out accident and firearm discharge reports. It's a good thing those Jeeps had medical kits. If you get a bunch of APs together, that means most of the silos weren't being patrolled at all. That's just dangerous and bad for morale. And some of those patrols would go far away from where they were supposed to be. If anything had happened, they wouldn't have been available.

"Some time ago, a wing commander tried to upgrade those patrols by having M60 machine guns mounted on the Jeeps and issuing each Air Police person two hand grenades. That was another bad idea. The AP was authorized to fire the M60 a few times at the start of their patrols to make sure it wasn't jammed. Apparently, the FNGs on patrol didn't know how far the M60 could shoot. Its max effective range was 3,609 feet. But its max *range* was 2.3 miles. So the AP teams ended up putting bullet holes through the Hueys delivering replacement crews to the silos for crew changeover on icy days. This pissed off the helicopter maintenance people to no end, and there was bad blood and even fistfights that broke out here and there. There were almost riots at the Memorial Day Wing Parade when helicopter Maintenance personnel flipped off the APs marching by.

"Maybe back in the heyday better communication would've prevented a lot of mistakes, but missiles was an entry level job in the military for a lot of people back then. People often didn't think and reacted to events emotionally. A bit more thinking might have solved problems early. I remember hearing about a missile security person assigned to three silos who drove 60 miles back to the city when he was supposed to be on patrol. He found his wife in bed with another Air Policeman and killed both of 'em with his M16. Sometimes, general, giving 19 year-olds weapons results in disaster rather than security. And that's what scares the hell out of me. Every crew member under your plan will feel 19 again. Even the crew commanders. So, who's really running the show? Some artificial intelligence somewhere? I'm inclined to accept your offer – a million dollars is a *lot* of money – but in all honesty, I think this plan is crazy. It sounds dangerous and irresponsible, sir. That's how I see it."

The general smiled and chuckled. "Robert, Robert…Don't get so upset. We know what we're doing and where we're going. It's okay. We're great managers. It's all being handled. We're confident we have a lid on everything. To our benefit, we've been able to save that technical knowledge in the veterans. And the new people get rapid, accelerated training. You see, we selectively erase recent memories. 'Selectively' is a loose term, but generally all memories within five years or so will be erased. That removes a lot of possible guilt one might feel about going away. There will be no contact at all with your current family for five years. You'll tell them you have a classified job offer – you can hint at the bonus or tell them outright – and that there's no contact for five years."

"If you decide to have a new life somewhere with Susan, we'll put you into what you'd essentially call a Witness Protection Program, and you'll have your new life with her. Your family will believe you were killed in an accident, and they'll collect your life insurance and partial pay for that month. They'll be taken care of. Or you can stay five years in the silo, then go back to your family and kids. That's up to you."

Robert made no effort to hide the suspicion in his voice. "Besides the missiles being armed and fueled, and an undisciplined crew of people who haven't pulled alert in years, if ever, what's the catch?"

"I already told you. The catch is no human contact except with the crew and official business. Absolutely none. We can't risk information about the 54 hidden silos getting out. No messages, no emails, no mail at all, no phone calls, no visitors. If you leave the silo, you forfeit your job. No going up to see the sky and sun as of now. Health teams and maintenance teams come to you through underground tunnels. They come and go. You don't. You stay for five years underground in the silo unless we change the policy to allow you topside. But you're never off the complex. And besides, we believe you'll want to stay there with your loved one and not have to endure a lot of questions, especially from the press."

"What if Susan and I break up?"

"She goes away. You stay. You get a new crewmember. A replacement."

Robert shook his head. "She can't really be Susan. She's a duplicate. A clone or something."

"Robert, she's Susan. Go do this job and she'll love you always. She wants a life with you. Lots of our employees never leave their silos, even after they've reached their five years. This is the closest thing to a perfect life the government can offer. Eat what you want, drink what you want, have hobbies and games. Study, read, whatever. Sleep. The silos are duplicates of the ones you served in. These silos – both the known and hidden ones – were all built at the same time. They're the same, down to the last detail. This is heaven on earth."

"You say that, but only knowing three people for five years…That doesn't sound like heaven to me. That's not much variety, to put it mildly. And being cooped up underground like that. No wind, no rain, no sunlight. Just concrete walls. For five years? People could go insane."

"There's certainly potential for stress, but you're getting paid generously for this. It's only 60 months. You can sleep when you want. There are no watches to stand and no set working hours. Someone has to monitor the equipment but that's about it. No drills. You already know how to launch the missile. The code procedures to prevent unauthorized launches are the same. Red box for the keys, two combo locks. You get some refresher training, but the likelihood of actually using the missiles is very low, and would be a last-ditch, fallback position. They'll probably never be used, but they're there if we ever need them."

Robert looked at the general with a somber expression on his face. "What if a person falls in love with the other person's mate?"

"Well, now, that's been a problem we've had to deal with at times. We can't deny that. We've had to deactivate a few crews and let all four people go. You'll just have to be content with your assigned partner, and so will the others. We can't overcome all human emotions, and turning people back to age 19 does tend to diminish some of the coping mechanisms they learned throughout their life. It's been a real problem, but we're on it. You can be assured of that. I should tell you that some crews have come to favor polygamy, but there was also a case where three out of the four crewmembers bonded, and the fourth got left out. The 'outcast' of the group sought revenge and ended up killing the other three crewmembers. He used one of the mil .38 specials stored in the silo in case of an attempted break-in. It was one of the worst tragedies we've ever experienced."

Robert stared intently at the photo of Susan. Eyes on him, in a bikini. She really did look as he remembered her at 19.

"I'll have to think about this," he said. "It may not be worth the money."

"Fair enough," the general replied. "That's for you to decide. Think about it and sleep on it. But take my advice and ask yourself: Is it worth the two of you having a life together – a life of love – for at least five years, and maybe longer? That's the real prize here. It's not the money, though that's a nice incentive. It's about being together again. A second chance for both of you."

"Did her life work out? Did she stay married?"

The general sighed. "I'm sorry, Robert. I can't discuss that, and she won't discuss her past life when you're together in the silo, assuming she remembers any of it. She'll never ask you about your life and what happened after she left you. It'll be as if the two of you never broke up, and you'll both be as happy as you used to be. You can pick up where you left off years ago. Who else gets that chance?"

Robert nodded and did his best to take in what the general had said. The room suddenly felt hot and stuffy, and he wanted to go home. "Just one more question, General. Those revolvers used to be in a locked cabinet, and they had no safeties. Is the gun cabinet in this dream-come-true silo locked, as well?"

"No, the revolvers aren't locked away. You can get to 'em quickly in case of emergencies, break-ins, that sort of thing. They're stored in the gray cabinet by the television lounge chairs, and they're loaded. Things are more relaxed in our silos. We've done away with lots of rules and nonsense. Everyone hated gun cleaning on Sunday, so we don't bother with that anymore. We changed it from once a week to once every six months. No point cleaning guns all the time if they're never used. We've really relaxed procedures based on the setting and circumstances. We're much more focused on the job now. Crews don't travel anymore, and there are no meetings or briefings, no vehicles, and no weekly gun cleanings. We use an old, reliable system, which means there are no tech order changes. No new classified materials. The 54 missiles we have are largely unaffected by time, and our system is very efficient. It really comes down to one decision: Do we launch today or not?"

Robert bristled. "But General, don't all those tasks keep people busy and focused? If there's little to do, what do crews do when they're on alert? There's only so much TV a person can watch, or books to read, or places to go online. Only so many hours a person can sleep or listen to music or play video games. So, what do crews really do for the half-decade they're down there?"

"They stay ready to launch upon receiving an order which can only come from the president. He doesn't know about these 54 hidden missiles, but he'd be debriefed if there were a crisis and made aware of them. As I said before, this gives him plausible deniability if the press started asking questions – which they would."

The general rose and handed Robert a card.

"Well, Robert, I enjoyed our chat. Call this number if you want the job. You have 30 days to think about this, and then you'll never hear from us again. We won't be here if you drop by in six months, and there'll be no record of us ever being here or having this conversation. We'll come back one time to meet you here if you're interested, and we won't stay long. That's the last day you'll see your family for five years, assuming you complete the assignment, so arrange your affairs and say goodbye to them. Thanks for coming by, Robert."

The two shook hands.

"Goodbye, General. I'll think on it carefully."

The general smiled. "I'm sure you will. Oh, and just in case you don't completely understand, here are some photos of what our rejuvenation project can do. This is your beloved Susan from long ago, before and after rejuvenation."

The general handed Robert an 8.5" x 11" sheet of glossy photo paper, with two captioned photos side by side. Robert looked at them intently.

NASS Rejuvenation Project, Subject 65. Susan. Location: 28.7031° N, 81.3384° W. Project Status: Successful.

The general smiled as Robert stood there in shock, then handed him another sheet of photo paper.

NASS Rejuvenation Project, Subject 14. Joseph. Location: 40.7440° N, 74.0324° W. Project Status: Successful.

The general's smile grew wider. "Pretty impressive, eh? That's Joseph, early in our rejuvenation project. The photos are in the same order as before: the first as he really was, then after we did our magic. Joseph's case is truly remarkable. He was a cooper, and his great-great-grandson is still living in northern New Jersey. NASS made him young again during a very early experiment. The pre-rejuvenation photo was taken in Brick, New Jersey, where he built a log cabin from pine. The after photo with him all dressed up was taken in Hoboken. We know how to make you and your loved one young again, Robert. These are real people, and these pictures are insurmountable proof of what we can do. I'll need them back before you leave, of course. Think on it and call the number I gave you if you decide to accept the offer. Enjoy the rest of your day."

Robert walked out the door, took the elevator down, and headed home. There was a lot to think about, but most of all, he remembered the scent of Susan's perfume and the taste of her in the front seat of his car long ago as a college student in New Hampshire.

Chapter 2: At Home in Connecticut

Robert sat across from his family at the kitchen table as they ate dinner. He'd spent a week thinking about the general's offer, and decided he'd bring it up this evening and see what everyone thought.

"I've been offered a new job, one that pays very well," he said as they sat around the table.

"Yes?" asked Sherry, his spouse. The kids looked bored, as usual.

"It's a lot of money but there's a catch."

"There always is," Sherry said.

"It means being away for five years." He didn't mention there was an option to stay even longer if he wanted.

Sherry took a drink of wine, sat the glass down, and looked at him. "We'd manage."

"You kids have anything to say?" Robert asked.

They were both silent and appeared bored by the discussion.

"If it means we can live better, I think you should do it," said his son. "You won't be gone forever. You'll be back."

"And you?" Robert asked his daughter.

"I'm okay with it," said Debbie. "I'm tired of never being able to get what I want when I go shopping, and looking lame when I go to school. I'm pretty sure all my friends think we're poor. It sucks."

There seemed to be no more discussion. His spouse, son, and daughter all looked bored. Beyond the financial side of things, there were no strong feelings about him leaving for 60 months. No drama, no grief, no resistance. Nothing.

"There's a salary," Robert informed them, "but the big bonus comes in five years if I stay that long."

A look of impatience came over Sherry's face. "Well, are you going to tell us what you'll be doing or do we sit here and wait?"

As Robert answered, he had the distinct feeling he wasn't really looking *at* his wife, but through her. *God, what a bitch,* he thought. *Let's get this over with.*

"I'd be working for the government," he said. "It's a classified project. A general I knew when I was on active duty offered it to me. He said I was an ideal candidate. I can't say much more than that, except I'm not allowed to communicate with any of you, and vice-versa, for five years. When those five years are up, we get one million dollars in non-taxable money. We're set for life, and I'll continue to draw retirement pay for the rest of my life, as well."

The three of them looked at him, their demeanor suddenly brightening.

"Holy shit, Dad," his son said. "A *million* dollars? Are you fucking serious? That's *life-changing* money. We wouldn't have to live in poverty anymore. That's fucking awesome!"

"We don't live in poverty, Ryan. We just--"

"I could shop wherever I wanted!" Debbie cried. "No more lame-ass clothes!"

Robert looked at Sherry and sighed. "Are you in favor of me doing this? Oh, there's another benefit. They do some sort of treatment, and I'll look much younger."

"Like plastic surgery?" Debbie asked.

"More like a combination of surgery, drugs, molecular rearrangement…lots of secret stuff. So you get a dad back who's a lot younger. Not just in appearance – I'll actually be younger."

"Sounds cool," Ryan said. "Go for it, Dad."

"It won't bother you not to see your dad for five years?"

"I mean, it sucks you'll be gone that long," Debbie replied, "but I think the benefits are worth more than us just sitting around being mad at each other half the time. We don't really have family time anymore besides dinner, and that's usually awkward. I say go for it."

They finished their meal and went their separate ways.

Later, lying in bed, Robert thought to himself: *I just as well go. The kids are growing up and have their own friends and interests. I have a spouse I'm not close to at all, and the money would improve all our lives. I'll make the call and get things in order. Besides, there's Susan. A 19-year-old Susan. Like she used to be. I can go back…*

And then he was asleep and at peace, dreaming of a time when so much of his life was still ahead of him, filled with hope.

Chapter 3: Rejuvenation

Robert arrived by taxi at the building where he'd met the general a week earlier. Everything looked the same when he arrived at the fifth floor. When he entered the office, however, a different civilian was in the anteroom and the door to the inner office was open with no one at the desk.

"Hello, Robert. I'm Colonel Tony Sampson, the general's aide. I'm a retired military serviceman, like him. I'm here to get the hiring process started. That's what we call it, anyway. I think of it more as a metamorphosis into a new life."

They shook hands.

"You wouldn't mind me seeing your ID card, would you?" Robert asked.

The colonel chuckled. "I'll do you one better. I'll show you *two* ID cards – one before rejuvenation, the other after. I keep the old one around for shits and giggles. What do you think?" Smiling, the colonel held his IDs up, side-by-side, for Robert to see. "I was Subject #256."

Robert looked carefully. They both looked real, each showing the rank of a retired Army colonel below the picture.

"It's incredible," Robert replied. "You look decades younger now. But I'll level with you, Colonel. I have serious concerns about the mental effects of this rejuvenation project. I don't think you can play around with the human brain without the potential for unintended consequences."

"I appreciate your concern, but we've got more than a few highly-respected academics monitoring the project. They urged caution, of course, but none of them said it was a flat-out bad idea. The general's going to press on unless there's solid evidence something's wrong. If that happens, we'll reevaluate and go from there."

"How did an Army man get involved with a USAF general? Seems like an unusual mix," Robert commented.

"I was a nuclear targeting officer working with Pershing missiles originally. It was an easy transformation to learn about your weapon system. The general and I met when he was in Hawaii. After he retired, he tracked me down and offered me a position in this civilian company with classified contracts. And now I help the new hires. I'll be with you through most of the process."

"How long does that take?"

"It takes some time. A lot of it depends on genetics. It's hard to say exactly, but you start getting paid today. Oh, before we go, one thing. You leave your cell phone, any weapons, and your watch here on the deck. They'll be stored until you leave. Any compasses stay here – some people have those little compass tie clips or bracelets. Leave them here if you have any."

"Where's our first stop?"

"Well, you won't be thrilled, but your first stop is a classified hospital run by the CIA. As the general told you, we're going to make you younger...a *lot* younger."

They walked to an elevator which took them to a parking garage, and headed toward a standard black government car. "You ride in the back," Tony said. "I drive."

Robert got in the back of the vehicle and sat down as Tony pushed a button that darkened the windows. "That's so you don't see where this place is," he said. "All very hush-hush, you know. The car is soundproof; it should be a very quiet and comfortable ride. Feel free to sleep if you'd like. It's about three hours down to Maryland. That's all I can tell you."

Tony was right. The ride was smooth and silent. There was no indication of where they were or how long they'd been traveling. The air seemed to have the scent of the ocean, and then Robert fell asleep, head back on the head rest. Just before doing so, a faint thought entered his mind: *I didn't want to fall asleep, but I'm going to. They drugged the air in here...*

He awoke in a hospital room into a fuzzy world of sunshine. There was a nurse nearby, all cheery and busy. He lay there trying to reconnect time and place to something, but couldn't do so. There was nothing to connect to. There seemed to be nothing in his mind at all except a feeling that the sun was warm outside. *Must be drugs,* he thought. He felt at peace not having anything to do, and thought of almost nothing. A face appeared and looked down at him.

"Good morning. I'm Doctor Rover. Can you tell me your name?"

"Robert."

"Good, that's right. Can you tell me what you remember?"

Robert thought as hard as he could, but there was nothing. He began to feel afraid.

"I can't remember anything. Was I in an accident?"

"No, no, don't be concerned," the doctor replied.

On Thursday, Colonel Sampson stopped by Robert's hospital room. There had, in fact, been no visitors after the surgical rejuvenation procedure and initial DNA injections. There were no mirrors in the room, so after a month of recovery and face bandages, it was time to view the results.

The colonel sat in a chair beside the bed where Robert was resting.

"You know, Robert, this procedure is experimental. Altering DNA code, facial injections, plastic surgery, and some out-of-this-world gravity-free procedures which are classified…this doesn't always result in a good outcome. In some cases, to put it mildly, the outcome was dismal. On some of our new employees, the procedure resulted in severe facial abnormalities for the rest of their lives. It was horrible."

"What happened to those people? Did they die?"

"Well, they all lived through the procedure. That was the good news. All of them retired from the project to a military-controlled island. It's near Fire Island. 'No Trespassing by US Government order.' They live their lives there in comfort and peace. Their families were taken care of."

"So that's it? They retired to a magical island?"

"Well, almost. The houses are restored 1890 homes. Very nice and elegant. Security guards keep trespassers out."

"And them *in*, I take it."

"Well, we thought it best."

"*You* thought it best, you mean. Right? Not 'we.' Just *you*."

The colonel sighed. "Yes, Robert, I thought it best, and so did the unnamed officers I report to."

"How many are on the island?"

"Some 242 people. Not one or two, or vast quantities. And not their families – just the 242 volunteers. They can live together or alone. They're provided with whatever they ask for."

"Sex?"

"If they're in the mood. Most aren't interested. And they won't have children…ever. That's an added benefit of the rejuvenation procedure. We didn't originally know that was one of the effects of the injections, but we eventually realized that was the case. Men and women come out of the rejuvenation treatments as perfectly sterile people. We're not exactly sure why, but it has something to do with altering their DNA. We don't know if the genetic alteration could be passed on to a child, but that's basically a moot point. So now we tell people beforehand that they won't be able to have kids. So far, that hasn't stopped anyone from going through with the procedure."

"And when do you know if the process worked or not?"

"I'd say as soon as we remove the bandages. It's like that old episode of *The Twilight Zone*. We've found it either worked or failed, and we're not sure why. There seems to be no middle ground with this. Either you like what you see in the mirror, or you don't. We've found that subjects have a strong reaction either way. Take a look at this. Impressive, isn't it?"

With that, the colonel handed Robert a sheet of glossy photo paper. It was an all-too-familiar move at this point, and Robert sighed as he looked at the photos.

NASS Rejuvenation Project, Subject 342. Mary. Location: 39.5299° N, 119.8243° W. Project Status: Successful.

The colonel cleared his throat. "Robert, there's something else you should know about the rejuvenation program. It's not just for older military veterans like you and me. We also have a good number of civilians who've participated in the program, at our invitation. They accepted a position with NASS, just as you did. In fact, about half the people in our program aren't veterans themselves, but civilians who know the veterans who accepted a position with us. Like you and Susan."

Robert stared at the colonel.

"I don't understand."

"Well, think about it, Robert. Would you want to be young when the people you were closest to in life were all old? Of course not. But how many of us would give anything to be young again with someone we loved, and have a second chance at life with that person? Mistakes from years ago could be repaired, and you could be with the person you were meant to spend your life with. A second chance at life and love."

"And if the process works for one person but not the other?"

"Then the other person is going to get their heart broken. That's a problem, obviously, and an area we need to do better in. Right now, there's no middle ground. It either works or it doesn't, and we're not sure why. But if it works, you'll be 50 years younger and have all those years to relive. You'll outlive your contemporaries, but you'll have that special someone with you. And you'll find new young friends like you did years ago. We give people something very few are ever offered. We can fix your broken heart so you can live and *love* again. That's really something – even for someone as skeptical as you."

Robert listened carefully, evaluating the colonel's words. "Okay, then. Now what?"

The colonel spoke in a somber, matter-of-fact voice. "Now we find out if it worked."

"Hmm," Robert muttered. "Tell me, Colonel, do you know the answer already? I'm pretty sure I know how this whole thing works. You warn people it could go wrong when you know it went right. Manage expectations. Never let people see a mirror if something went wrong. Just whisk them off to some unknown island, away from society. And you already know about my match, don't you? If this doesn't work, you have a list of people to go through until it does. Then you pair the people it worked for. Am I right?"

The colonel smiled benignly.

"Well, you got me. It does go along pretty much as you described. We do have a list of special people, and fortunately, the process worked on the first candidate for you. Two other women on our list of probable matches for you, both of whom you knew a long time ago, died from cancer. You won't have to worry about that, and neither will Susan."

"So she knew this would result in us getting back together?"

"Absolutely. She wants a second chance at life with you. You two are the perfect match. But first, you can see how young you are."

He called out for an aide, and several people came in: doctors, technicians, a nurse, and others. The nurse, wearing an RN ID, removed Robert's face and neck bandages. He looked in the mirror one of the civilians was holding for him. He indeed was young. No gray, no lines. He looked 20 again. The procedure had worked so far, except for one thing.

"I look young, but why don't I feel any different? I still feel 70. Tired and old."

"No worries. We'll fix that in a minute. When we first started this project, it took us a while to realize it's a two-step process. Appearance first, then we fix the aged cells so you *feel* young, too. Soon, you'll have the stamina and drive you had at 20. In fact, the change is so overwhelming that some people need therapy to deal with it. Do you even remember what it was like to be 20 years old?"

There was no reply.

"I didn't think so."

One of the doctors brought over a chilled aluminum box with frost on the outside. The box was secured with two padlocks. A doctor unlocked one, and Colonel Sampson unlocked the other.

"You'd think this was gold that way it's safeguarded," Robert commented. "What's in the box?"

"Oh, it's much more valuable than gold. See for yourself."

Robert opened the lid, and there, nestled in padding, was an oversized syringe, red liquid inside, that ended with a long, thin needle.

"For me?"

"Yes. It's a very special plasma made in zero gravity from the converted blood of Susan. In your case, she did the procedure first and it worked, as you know. Your blood type is compatible with hers. Things need to go well for the first person of a pair, and less so for the second. It doesn't have to be perfect to work for you. It does for her."

"And there's a top-secret lab that produces this plasma?"

The colonel chuckled. "Indeed. It's on board the Space Station, if you can believe it. People have no idea what we're producing up there, and that's obviously a good thing."

"Why protect it so?"

The colonel scoffed. "Come on, Robert. You know the answer to that. Imagine what would happen if anyone else discovered this. People who could afford it would get it; poor and middle-class people wouldn't. Nations would go to war over this. And suppose it were perfected where people could live and be young for hundreds of years. Imagine if Einstein could keep turning back the clock, or Henry Ford. Imagine the repercussions. There'd be food shortages, overpopulation, crowding, social problems like we've never seen before. There'd be worldwide chaos. For now, we try it on a few people and continue studying it. We really don't know why the procedure works, so we're trying to learn."

"You'll be studying me and Susan?"

"As much as we reasonably can, yes. For example, will you still age at the same human rate? Will the two of you age at the *same* rate? Will you get along better than years ago? There's a lot to answer and research. The big payoff is your broken heart will be healed and like new. You'll get the life together you should've had for all these years."

"Do you think it's possible we won't get along?"

"It's possible…but very unlikely. We've thoroughly investigated your personalities. Put it this way: There's better than a 90% chance the two of you will be happy together. For a lifetime. Hell, we're not even sure when you'll die, but it's probable that whenever that occurs, your deaths will be close to each other. We don't know how long you'll live, but we assume it'll be 'til around 80 or so. We also don't know if the process can be repeated on the same couple over and over. Wouldn't that be something?"

They were both silent a minute. The colonel then asked everyone but the RN to leave the room. Robert wondered if they were being filmed, then realized he really didn't care. This, he reminded himself, could be one of the most incredible journeys ever taken by a human being. To cheat time, reset the clock, and be his younger self again.

"Well, here we go. Sorry, Robert. This shot goes in your butt, not your arm. Works better that way."

He handed the syringe to the RN and left the room.

"Bend over the bed, please, and hold still," she said. "This takes 30 seconds to complete."

She opened his hospital gown and slowly injected the plasma. When finished, she dropped the empty syringe in a disposal box on the wall.

"Now what?" Robert asked.

"Sit here by me and wait. My name is Cindy. I'm a psychotherapy emergency room RN. You might need me. You'll feel hot, then might not remember much of anything until eight hours have passed. Your brain is about to return to the past. Much of your life that occurred after 20 years of age may vanish. You are truly going to feel 20 again, with most of your life still ahead of you. I'm here to keep you calm and comfortable. People are often skeptical when it comes to something as incredible as this, but the staff here really care about you and your well-being."

"I don't feel like myself," Robert said. "I feel…I don't know. *Disconnected,* I guess."

"It's okay," Cindy assured him. "That's normal. Here…I have a surprise for you. How's a walk on the beach sound?"

A photo of Cindy taken at Illinois Wesleyan University.

She reached into a backpack and took out bathing suits for the two of them.

"Go change in the bathroom while I change here, and I'll show you one of many things about this project you're gonna love."

When he finished changing, she stood up from the bed, barefoot, wearing a black bikini. She looked stunning in a bikini versus her Army nurse's uniform. She looked at him and smiled, her eyes bright with excitement.

"You won't need shoes. Let's go through that door. It's mini-vacation time."

He'd tried the door once, but it had been locked. Now she opened it for him, and they walked beneath some palm trees toward a lagoon. The sun was setting, the water turning silver under the full moon, the sand white and gold. As far as they could see, the water stretched to the horizon. There was no one else but the two of them. The water made lapping sounds on the sand, nighttime critters made noises, and birds flew in front of the rising moon. His brain felt as if it were made of Jell-O sent falling from a kitchen table. He felt as if he were tilted to the right while walking. Of course, this wasn't real; it was a room in a military science research center that used projection devices, sound, color, sand, real water, and temperature controls to make the illusion *seem* real. They waded knee-deep in the warm water, which seemed, Robert thought, to perfectly match his body temperature, making him feel one with his surroundings.

"Come with me," she said. "It's safe here in the water. No monsters or fish or anything else; just us."

She led him deeper into the lagoon until the water was up to her chest.

The calm, relaxing water buoyed Robert in a way that made him feel like he was floating in the air, and he stared at the moonlight shining off its surface. Cindy floated in front of him, then stood with her arms around him, pulling him toward her. He could feel the sand beneath his feet and see bats flying in front of the full moon. As beautiful as it was, he felt as if he couldn't remember anything. Not his name, where he was, or what he planned to do tomorrow. He couldn't remember anyone or anything, and he began to feel nervous and apprehensive. He suddenly felt like screaming and running ashore. His brain hunted for something – anything – to remember, but found nothing. His hands on her shoulders were shaking now, and he felt as if he were falling into the dark, empty spaces between the moonlit water. The dark lagoon seemed to draw him under, and he felt as if he were toppling uncontrollably. A woozy, disorienting feeling took hold of him, and his brain suddenly felt like it was wobbling around in his skull.

Cindy placed her hands firmly on the sides of his neck, massaging him gently. "Robert, look at me. There's nothing and no one to fear. I promise you. Not me, or the colonel, or anyone here. There's nothing in the water except us. I want you to breathe deeply. Stop panting and hold me against you. You're shaking. Are you cold? Put your hands on my hips and hold me against you. Are you afraid of something?"

Robert shivered in her arms. "I'm afraid of this project. The outcome. Government projects always end badly. I saw it over and over when I was on active duty. The more people say, 'It's a great project,' the greater the damage when everything implodes. Why would this be any different? This project is attempting to rewrite the entire behavior, beliefs, and biology of humans. That can only be done in increments, not in one big hunk of transformation. What if this ends in tragedy and everything falls apart?"

Cindy tilted her head toward the ceiling.

"Amanda, are you with us tonight?"

A soft, synthetic voice replied: "Yes, Cindy. How can I help you?"

"Amanda, increase the water temperature by 15 degrees Fahrenheit, and turn on the underwater lighting, color blue."

The computer made the requested changes.

Amanda (AI). Self-generated image.

Robert's surprise at hearing an unexpected voice was strong enough to stop his shaking. "We're not alone in here? But you said –"

"It's just Amanda. She's a computer, not a person. Artificial intelligence. She fixes things, and she's very good at it. She's a special fourth-generation computer built by another computer and overlaid with its personality and voice tones. She wasn't built from a kit. She's actually a descendant from a computer we nicknamed 'The Cook' because she's always cooking up ideas for NASS and its programs. She's another defense project we incorporated with our rejuvenation project. It's not just computers building computers. It's passing down the original voice and personality traits generation after generation, with modifications done by the computers themselves. Sort of like genes are inherited from one person to the next. Anyway, do you really want to discuss DoD research when you have me in your arms?"

She was as tall as he was, thus making it easy for their lips to meet.

Chapter 4: Susan

Robert awoke in a different hospital bed. He felt a sense of peace and comfort he hadn't felt in quite some time. He tried to remember what had happened after the injection but could only recall fragments of what he'd seen and felt in the hours that followed: smooth thighs, warm lips, an endless beach under a full moon, her looking down at him, hands on his chest, a great letting go of loneliness and bitterness that had been his life for years with no special person to share it with.

Robert lay still, feeling no needs at all. The nurse came by; her name tag read "Betsy," and she gave him an injection. When he awoke again, it was nighttime. There were lights outside his window, and his bedside lamp was on. He was in a different room, more like an apartment than a hospital room.

A visitor greeted him. "Hello, Robert. I'm Dr. Melanie Mullen. I'm head of Neurological Surgery here at the hospital. This is a higher-level hospital than the one before, Top Secret as far as projects go. We specialize in brain surgery and neurological pathways of memories. Basically, we alter and enhance your brain through surgery. It's an exciting field to practice in, and I'm very happy you're here."

Robert stared at her blankly. "Why am I here? Did something happen to me?"

"You're a new employee in a government program, and we've done some rejuvenation surgeries and chemical treatments. Memories will come back. We'd be more alarmed, actually, if you remembered a lot, since a major part of the process is to turn back the clock, remove unpleasant memories, and save the happier ones earlier in your life. We thought you were a good candidate when we hired you, and the fact you don't remember much is a very good sign. Try to rest and get some sleep. I'll have the nurse give you something to let you sleep if you're tired, which I assume you are. I'll see you when you wake up again."

When Robert awoke again, the nurse checked his vital signs and an aide brought him breakfast consisting of apple juice, a toasted bagel, scrambled eggs, and heart-healthy (i.e., tasteless) turkey bacon.

The door opened, and Robert watched as Colonel Sampson walked in and sat by the bed. "Hi, Robert. You feeling more awake? You like your new room?"

"Yes. I seem to be more alert. Where am I?"

"You're in another government hospital in Maryland. It's a classified facility. Not open to the public. There are other people like you here, all going through the same rejuvenation process. You'll be here awhile to get your mind back together, go through tests, and maybe relearn some memories. But we've gotten pretty good at this over the years, so I doubt you'll need much help with your memories."

"I'm not so sure. My mind's completely blank at the moment."

"Don't worry. It'll come back. We've tried to erase the more recent, less happy memories while retaining the happier ones from when you were younger."

"You can be that time specific?"

"More or less. Recent memories are stored in one area of the brain while older, long-term memories are stored in another. We modify the recent area and leave the long-term area alone. Those older memories will come back. The recent ones – those within the last 20 years, give or take – won't come back. We can't get down to specific days or months at this point in the project – only years."

Robert felt the slightest sense of unease. "None of my recent memories will come back?"

"Only a few, perhaps. It's not absolute, but they won't pain you anymore. Indebtedness, emotional pain, loneliness, memories of aging…they'll be mostly gone since these are more recent memories in all our new employees. It's one of the common characteristics of our new hires, most of whom served in the military. Their older memories are always happier and better than their recent ones. With the rejuvenation project, we keep the good ones and let the bad ones go, and give people a do-over at life."

"Aging. I remember some discussion about that, but I can't remember the conversation or the person I talked to."

"You talked with a General Birmingham about that. Do you remember him?"

"A little. We talked about active duty, I believe. But that was a long time ago."

The colonel smiled. "Actually, you talked with him about that just three months ago. You see, Robert? That memory is mostly gone. That's just a sample of what we did. I bet you feel very calm right now. That's a side effect we've discovered with the procedure. The general is coming to see you soon. You're going to discover you're a lot younger. It's not just memories. We redid you. Top to bottom."

Robert thought a minute. "Did I agree to all this?"

"Oh, yes. Of course. Would you like to see the video?"

"No, that's okay." He lay quietly, then asked, "Can I get up?"

"If you want to. I'll get the nurse to help. You may be a bit unsteady for a while since you haven't used them much recently. No worries, though. You'll get rehab therapy to get you back in shape."

"I feel really weird, like something's missing."

"Well, something *is* missing. It's your memories. Many are gone, as I explained. We took away the recent ones. Try to remember the last thing you did."

Robert thought a bit, then said, "I think it was my Air Force duties. I think so, but I have a feeling that's wrong."

"Okay, so this is a good example. To you, that was the last thing you did, and it seems recent. That's what we hoped for, since it means you still have all your technical knowledge."

"Hmm. Okay, then. What *don't* I remember?"

The colonel chuckled. "Now Robert, the whole point was to turn the clock *back*. If I tell you what you *don't* remember, it might bring everything back, which defeats the purpose. In your new job with us, you'd find those old memories cumbersome and useless anyway."

"I don't even know what my new job is or whom I work for."

"Your work for NASS, Inc. Your old friend, General Birmingham, serves as Director of Crew Preparation, among many other positions. We do important, classified work for the U.S. military. My name is Tony, and I'm the general's assistant."

"Is the general my friend? Really?"

"Absolutely. He's a friend to everyone, everywhere, involved in the defense of America."

"What will I be doing in this job?"

"You're going back on ICBM nuclear missile alert duty, somewhat modified from what you remember. But the system is still the same. You'll get some refresher training, of course. As for now, you're welcome to try to get out of bed, enjoy the view, and get some rest. You'll have physical therapy later this afternoon."

Robert looked around at his room. There was no TV and no mirrors.

"Why no mirrors?" he asked. "I get how watching TV could mess with my memories right now, but why no mirrors?"

"Well, Robert, it's something of a shock for patients to see how young they look immediately after rejuvenation. Trust me – you look much, *much* younger than before. Best to wait a few days so you're not overwhelmed. Remember: It's not just the surgeries and plasma injection. It's not just your brain, either. Everything about you is 50 years younger now. Your attitude, energy, libido, stamina, confidence, assertiveness…everything."

Robert nodded. He had the odd feeling one has when they believe they're missing something, but don't know what it is. Something just out of reach, unable to be articulated.

"What if I want my old memories back? Can the process be undone?"

"We've had some success in bringing memories back."

"It's difficult to make decisions now that we've started. You said I wanted this?"

"You certainly did. We recorded you discussing this project, remember? If you want to see the recordings, I'd be happy to –"

"No, that's okay. I trust you, and for the most part, I trust the goals of the US government. If you say I wanted this, there must've been a reason."

"Indeed. A very good one."

"Hmm. Money?"

"No, nothing so typical as that."

"Was it fame, then? Fortune, glory…none of the common reasons people do things?"

"No. Perhaps we shouldn't' discuss this. At least not now. It might make you think too much. Coping with everything involved in the rejuvenation process can be very difficult. You need to pace yourself. There'll be plenty of time to sort everything out."

"What's there to cope with?" Robert asked.

"Oh, goodness. All sorts of things for most people. I suspect you're no different. You may have old, conflicting emotions about Susan, doubts about your life, confusion as to why she did this for you…the list goes on and on."

"Is it that shocking to see someone again after so long?"

"It can be. It depends if we got the time lapse and memories under control. We've gotten much better at this. If all went well, you'll feel as if only a week has passed since you saw Susan. Otherwise, it'll seem as if she stood still and you had experiences and moved on. We'll know the answer soon. For now, get some rest and be well."

A knock on the door a few days later brought an aide with a USAF uniform complete with ribbons and lieutenant colonel rank, breakfast set on the table by a waiter in a white coat, and a message. "Sir, Colonel Sampson sends his regards and requests that you be ready for the next stage of your rejuvenation in one hour. You'll find shaving equipment in the latrine. The colonel hopes you slept well."

"Wait," Robert said as the aide turned to leave. "Can I see the RN who was here? The one I went on the beach with. We went through that door there."

The aide replied, "I'm sorry, sir. I don't know of any RN assigned to this research unit. And that door leads to a closet."

He opened the door and, indeed, a closet was there.

"Sir, you'll want to get ready. The colonel will be calling for you. Have a good day, sir." The aide nodded and left the room.

At exactly 10 a.m., the colonel arrived with General Birmingham. Robert was ready.

"Good morning, Robert. I stopped in to make sure you're doing well and being treated fairly."

"Yes, General. I'm coming along."

"Good, good. I'll be watching for your first alert." The general shook hands with Robert and departed.

Robert looked at the colonel and smiled. "So, I get to meet my significant other, I take it."

"Oh, yes. You sure do. I'm glad you survived your post-injection experience. Some volunteers have a rough time. You look pretty rested."

"I feel as if I'm living in multiple time zones. Colonel, is there any way I could talk to the RN who gave me the injection? I'd really like to see her again. I know she was real."

"Robert, I won't deny Cindy's existence, but seeing her now is a bad idea. Let it go. Besides, you're going to meet someone much more important."

They walked outside, lesser ranked saluting them, then away in the colonel's car to the Morris Hotel two miles away down a two-lane macadam road lined with trees. They went into a video conference room with a screen and eight chairs around a large table. Tony shut the door.

"Sit wherever. We're going to look at some slides and then take a little walk."

The first slide showed a couple by a VW beetle. The second showed the same couple dressed for a formal dance, he in a suit and she in a long blue gown. The third slide showed the couple playing in the snow with a mountain behind them. They were making snow angels. The fourth was of the two riding an old carousel in Hershey, Pennsylvania. The fifth was the two of them on the lawn outside an old college building. The sixth was them in line at the dining hall. Next was a beach shot, he in a black bathing suit and she in a purple one-piece suit. The eighth photo was the two of them holding hands, sitting in a church pew in Sunday clothing. The ninth was taken in front of her parents' house in Pennsylvania with her, Robert, and her family. The final photo was a closeup of her face, her freckles showing clearly, the reddish tint to her hair shining in the afternoon sun.

Tony shut off the projector. "Ready to go?" he asked Robert.

"Where did you get those photos from?"

"Your mind, while you were unconscious. Same technology as getting those videos from your mind. We hoped these might make the past more real to you. Make you feel less anxious."

Robert stared at him, suddenly realizing that the time spent going through procedures and orientation had all come to this. "Maybe we should wait a day or two more," he said.

"It won't get easier. Once you two are alone, it'll be as if you saw each other a few days ago. You just have to walk into a room, and there she'll be. This is what you wanted all your adult life, Robert. To be with her. Well, she's *here*, and you can have that life together."

"I understand, but I still think I should wait a few days until I recover more. We shouldn't rush something that's taken years for NASS to achieve." The anxiety Robert felt moments ago was steadily increasing, and the room seemed to be tilting over to the right.

"Robert, have a seat," the colonel said, his voice calm and soothing. As he finished speaking, he took out a pill bottle and shook three blue pills into Robert's hand.

"What are those?"

"Neuron inhibitors. Stops you from being afraid or concerned about things. We call them bravery pills. Here, try three. You'll feel fine in a few seconds. They're very fast-acting. Remarkably fast. They're from another classified project."

Robert took the pills. "Well, there was nothing to be concerned about at all, was there?" he commented to Tony a few minutes later. "Nothing at all."

They took the elevator to the third floor. The hotel hall ended at a door marked "Suite 300" and Tony stopped. Two MPs stood in the hallway outside.

"Gentlemen, all okay here?"

"Yes, sir. All routine. She's in the suite."

Tony nodded. "You two can wait in the hall lobby; I'm going down to the main lobby for a newspaper. Let's let these two meet. It's been a long time coming." He turned to Robert as the two MPs departed. "Well, this is it. Welcome to your new life with Susan. She's expecting you. When you're ready, just knock on the door, walk in, and you'll be with her again. Order whatever you want from room service. Enjoy your time together. Good luck to you, Robert."

Tony walked back up the hall, leaving Robert standing by the door. He felt no anxiety as he knocked, opened the door, and walked into a living room. Susan was there, looking out the window at the lawn and trees. She turned to him, revealing freckles and a page boy haircut. Loafers, tight jeans, t-shirt. Makeup and earrings. He remembered more than he would've thought possible after so many years. Running in the snow, horse riding in October, country and western concerts, formal ROTC dances, birthday dinners at the Coach and Four restaurant, engagement rings. To see her here, to know her plasma was in his veins, that they had both succeeded in getting 50 years of their lives back to relive together…He was overwhelmed with a sense of awe and astonishment at the whole situation.

He walked over to her and stopped, not knowing what to say or do. She took his hands in hers and put them on her hips. "Don't look so shy," she said with a smile. "It hasn't been that long. I'm here, just as we both wanted."

He tried to make some sort of logical reply, but what came out sounded more like gibberish.

"Are you really you?" he finally managed.

"Well, who else would I be?" she replied with a laugh. "Don't you remember me?"

"Well, yes, it's just, just that it seems as if you haven't aged at all."

"It hasn't been that long, silly. I didn't age that fast. Ask me anything. You'll see that I'm me."

He thought for a minute.

"Okay. I'll ask, you answer. What's your favorite drink?"

"Cherry vodka. Remember when I dropped that full bottle outside the Sleepy Valley Motel?"

"Oh my, I'd forgotten about that. How about this: What's your favorite store?"

"The Golden Rule department store."

"What did you dad do when we were watching TV at your house?"

"He always left the room so we could be alone."

"What color swimwear do you like best?"

"Purple."

"Where did we eat on the first date?"

"The Coach and Four on Route 33. It burnt down."

"Turn your head to the right."

She did so, and he brushed back her hair to find the little scar behind her ear from when she fell off her bike as a child.

"You didn't think that scar would be there, did you? Now do you believe I'm me?"

"You don't wonder if I'm really me?"

"No, I know it's you. Tony told me about your unhappy life and how you wanted me back. Not a lot of people get this chance they've given us. To go back in time and find your true love. We get to do that."

"You wanted this too?"

"I did. Much more than the life I was living. The pay is outstanding, and we get to spend half a decade together. And who knows, we may end up staying together after that. I'm sure Tony told you some couples stay in this life together."

"He did."

They opened a bottle of black cherry merlot that had been cooling in a wine bucket.

"Nice of Tony to arrange a little alone time for us before we head to the silo," Robert said.

"Here's to us and a new life underground," Susan replied as she tapped her glass to Robert's.

"So what happens after dinner?" he asked.

"What do you think? We have the presidential suite for the night. It's free. President Eisenhower used the desk there to draft a military treaty. Looks as if the government or some agency is paying for everything tonight. We'll have to tell Tony thanks when we see him again."

"He's probably making sure we really are compatible before we go underground," Robert said. "That's a smart idea."

She took his hand. "Robert, I won't ask again. Do you ever think of your kids and the previous life you had anymore?"

"No. They're part of a different lifetime. It's already gone from my mind. The hypnotist at the project worked with me a lot so I could set them aside mentally and focus on you and the job. We really have a live missile down the hall. We have duties to perform and work to do down in the silo. It won't be all fun for five years. I hope those retired maintenance weenies know their stuff."

"Oh, I'm sure they do. This whole project seems to have its act together. I'm impressed. Now, come sit. Seeing it's me they chose must've been a surprise to you. It was a long time ago."

Robert nodded as he sat down beside her. "I never forgot you. I always hoped you'd come back. All my life I hoped you'd return." He tried to keep his tone logical, which proved very difficult. His mind felt a thousand miles away on vacation somewhere. It was like looking up at the side of a cruise ship from water level, where there's no perspective except awe and disbelief.

"Well, here I am. And no, I don't think about my prior life either. I think about us and the next five years. The million dollars and retirement benefits sound pretty good, too. We can stay together for the rest of our lives if we want. We can also stay with Titan or the rejuvenation project after our five years are up. Those two other missile jobs were enlisted jobs. Missile Facilities Technician and Ballistic Missile Analyst Technician. I guess we're getting two veterans or recent trainees in those jobs, and they've been rejuvenated, too.

"You probably don't know but I enlisted in the Air Force after college, went through Officer Candidate School, and was commissioned. I don't have any missile time. I was a communications equipment officer in a communications group. Big unit, 500 enlisted, most of them temporary duty."

Robert listened with interest. "Your active-duty time was a long time ago, too. Did you stay the 20 years in?"

"No, I left after the mandatory five I owed for going through OCS. I thought about becoming a military dentist, but the time commitment was too much on top of the five years I already owed the government. So I left and went into business banking. After a few years of low-level jobs, the pay was pretty good, even for women. I understand that people are selected for this program not just because they're vets, but because they're more flexible when it comes to following rules, and they don't like bosses or society. Rebels with a cause." She chuckled.

"That sounds about right," Robert replied. "I don't like neatness or order or bosses. I like jobs where I can make my own decisions and not have bosses watching my every move like a hawk. Missiles was the perfect job for me. I was at the wing alternate command post. So, if the base were destroyed, the ACP would manage the missile wing. And since the wing was the host unit, we also managed the Reserve unit refueling aircraft. The base included an air refueling wing. I was always reading the war plans in case the ACP had to manage things. But that never happened."

"I'm like that, too. I don't like being bossed around and told what to do or what to wear, or what to think. I haven't changed much since high school. I just wanna have fun."

They both smiled. There was a knock at the suite's door, and they welcomed the colonel in while the MPs waited outside.

"Nice of you to stop by, Colonel."

"Just wanted to see how you're doing," Tony replied. "I think the two of you should get well-acquainted. Spend the day together. I'm sure you have lots of catching up to do. I'll be back at 0900 tomorrow, and we'll go from there. There'll be two guards outside with rotating shifts every hour. A company of MPs is also nearby."

"Food?"

"Order room service. You'll have years to cook for each other. Enjoy being pampered tonight. I'm off to see some others in the program. I'll see you two tomorrow."

They said goodbye as the colonel left the room. Closing the door behind him, Susan turned to Robert with a look of excitement. "You heard the man. It's room service time. Going out's not an option, apparently. We'll just have to make do with each other and being waited on hand and foot."

They placed their order for room service: chef's salad with chicken and a cheese platter appetizer, cheesecake with strawberry ice cream, and butter cookies for Robert, while Susan ordered a cheese omelet and waffles with a side of hash browns and strawberries, and creme brulee for dessert.

"Robert, are you afraid of the past or the future?"

There was no hesitation in his answer. "The future. This program assumes the past can just be erased from our minds. But our personalities are products of that past, good or bad, so our past will always be part of our existence. I don't see how we can completely start over. What if those memories they've chemically suppressed start coming back at some point? I don't buy this nonsense about plasma injections from one person to another. I think we're being injected with a cocktail of chemicals that affects the mind. And I'd assume we're being watched in here. I'd be surprised if we weren't."

Susan's reaction was nonchalant. "I suppose so, but does it really matter? We'd behave the same way anyhow. No sense in overthinking things."

There was a pause.

"You do know we're spending the night together," she said.

"It seems that way. You want me to see if the guards will let me go back to the hospital?"

"Don't be silly. This place has everything. They even brought pajamas for us. Red for you, purple for me. My favorite color."

"It always was. How'd they know?"

"I have no idea. Hypnosis maybe. A doctor once told me I was susceptible."

She held out her hand.

"Don't be bashful. We slept together every weekend in high school. Come with me."

In the bedroom, sure enough, there were pajamas laid out neatly. Wine in an ice bucket on a night table. Lights dimmed. Pink roses placed throughout the room.

"It gets better."

"How?" Robert asked, cracking a smile. "Did the colonel give us one of those beds you put a quarter in and it shakes? They used to have those in every Route 30 motel in Pennsylvania."

Susan laughed. "Even better. We got a hot tub large enough for eight people. It's *huge*. They've got wall screens for it, and music with colored lighting. There's a whole menu. I've never seen anything like it."

Robert smiled and nodded. "I bet this is the colonel's work. This seems like his forte. Which nation do you think originally built it?"

"Who cares? It's ours tonight. I wonder if we get to use it *every* night."

"No doubt someone will want it back in the morning. Maybe if they get enough X-rated videos of us, they'll let us use it more often."

"Do you think we get to sleep together every night like this 'til we go to the missile silo?"

Robert shook his head. "I try not to guess too much when it comes to government projects. That way, I'm not wrong or disappointed as often. And God knows if this project is successful, it could alter mankind forever. But big projects like this rarely turn out like they're supposed to. There's always some flaw at some point, and shit happens. I just hope this is the exception."

She dimmed the lighting more.

"Do you still have that tattoo?" he asked.

"The cat on the shoulder with the green eyes?"

"That's the one. Still there?"

"Come over here and see for yourself."

"That means taking off your top."

"I guess it does, doesn't it? Think you remember how?"

"Some things you don't forget," Robert said as he undressed.

"Come shower with me, then we'll get in the play tub. The water feels amazing, so don't be shy. If they're going to record us, let's give 'em a show."

She sat on the plastic bottom with the water chest-high, back against the side, with him beside her. She laid her head on his shoulder, her hand over his. "You seem very moody about all this," she said to him. "Are you having regrets?"

"No. No regrets. It's amazing having a second chance at youth and love and a good, happy life. I hope I don't seem ungrateful. I'm just baffled why NASS chose us and wants to study us. We're just average kids who split up. Then we get picked to become young again, and to man an active, outdated missile silo armed with a nuclear warhead. From what the general said, there are 54 secret, hidden silos and we're just one of many teams in charge of them. But the government doesn't need us to man those silos. They could use active-duty people, make the project Top Secret, and save a lot of money in the process. So why us?"

Susan thought for a moment, then sighed. "I honestly have no idea. All I know is we have the whole night ahead of us. I was here last night, and this place is amazing. Let's just enjoy it and let the big questions wait. We've both waited decades for this night."

"You're right," Robert said while thinking of a walk on the beach with someone.

She fiddled with the selections on the jacuzzi menu, and the room slowly changed. It was now a sunny afternoon in a warm stream that flowed to the distant ocean. Georgia, he guessed. There were minnows in the stream and swans paddling past. One of them shook its wings and a feather fell out and floated by Robert, who picked it up.

He couldn't believe it: The feather was real. The sky darkened a bit and a few drops of rain fell, then stopped. The rainwater was salty, from the ocean. The minnows appeared three dimensional, their gills moving. The bottom became sand, with pebbles in the deeper middle of the stream. They weren't plastic, but actual rock pebbles.

Robert let out a sigh, overcome with awe. "We could be in a stream in Georgia on a July afternoon."

"We *are* in a stream in Georgia, Robert. It *is* July. Don't you see? It's all *real.* If you believe it, it's real. You just held a real feather and a real pebble, didn't you?"

"But it's only Georgia in this room."

"It's what you believe it to be. That's what matters. *We're* in this room. You and me. *Together.* Am I not real?"

"Yes, you are."

"And won't I still be real when we're in bed?"

"Yes."

"So why can't Georgia be right outside our bedroom door?"

He didn't know – nor want to know – the answer. Sometimes it's just better to believe and not overthink things.

He lay back, letting the warm water flow over him. A butterfly meandered by; it looked perfectly real. Maybe the hot tub was a blend of the real and the imagined. Maybe the imagined part seemed more real due to the bird feather and other tidbits of reality sprinkled in. In any case, it was a very comfortable place to be.

Chapter 5: Sandy and Jeffrey

Susan's hunch about them being together for their training turned out to be true. They lived at the hotel as long-term guests, and the kitchen and dining room proved very handy. Hotel staff did the daily housekeeping, giving them more time to study an array of military manuals. T.O. 21M- LGM25C-1 was the primary technical order to understand, but there were also reviews of electrical systems, water systems, hydraulics, guidance, launch procedures, troubleshooting procedures, communication equipment and procedures, launch sequence, propellent transfer system, hazard sensing, maintenance ground equipment, and a slew of others. Having been in the Titan II system previously, Robert remembered much of the procedures, though his knowledge of equipment troubleshooting wasn't as good. Susan, having no previous experience with Titan II, had everything to comprehend. They were so tired from studying that they often fell asleep immediately after dinner. They never met the other students, which they presumed was to get them oriented to having little social interaction for the five years they'd be in the silo. Finally, after numerous days of the same routine, they met the other two members of their crew: Sandy and Jeffrey.

Like Robert, Jeff had experience in Titan II from decades ago. Sandy had been educated on Titan as part of NASS's orientation program. Both had completed the rejuvenation process. They were in the academic building tech order library when Robert and Susan came to meet them. They all helped themselves to coffee in the lounge area, happy to have a break from their studies.

Sandy (photo taken in Gillette, New Jersey) and Jeffrey (photo taken in Rome, New York).

Robert started things off.

"Well, we're finally together. I hope you're both looking forward to this as much as you're probably enjoying the effects of the rejuvenation process. The colonel told me that, for the next phase of training, we'll be together on a simulator for a few days. It'll be four hours a day learning about maintenance assistance, launch actions, and troubleshooting problems. They want to see if we can handle the monotony of five years in a silo, and if we can maintain discipline and order if we're ever called upon to launch the missile."

"Are we going four-on and four-off like a standard alert for the five years?" Sandy asked.

"Probably not during the days when we're all around," Robert replied, "but yes when the MFT and BMAT are doing the daily shift verification, and at night, when two of us are asleep. The other two should be on level 2, keeping watch. This equipment is so outdated it'll take a miracle to get that missile out of the ground and into the sky. We'll be lucky if a leak doesn't kill us."

"But Robert, the entire complex has been refurbished and upgraded by an approved contractor," Jeffrey commented.

"Rather like putting wheels on grandparents and assuming they'll be wagons. Can't change a zebra's spots," said Robert.

"Well, anyway, we finish up our simulator time and head for the real silo soon. Then we start counting down our five years for a million dollars."

"Tell us, Robert, how are you planning on spending your million?"

Robert chuckled. "I'll spend it on getting old, I guess. Put enough aside for assisted living so I never have to worry about things. What about you, Sandy?"

"I'm gonna vacation like mad and party my brains out."

"Susan?"

"I'm thinking marriage and two kids. A good, normal, stable life. That's the life for me. And you, Jeffrey?"

"Well, I'm kind of an odd duck, I guess, but I'd love to teach Cold War history. It's fascinating how MAD has kept nuclear peace all these years by threatening the end of life on earth. And now some nations insist that a nuclear WWIII can be won. Maybe they're right – but what would be left of our society? I think that'd be a fascinating course to teach at a local college."

The others nodded in agreement.

"Well," Robert said, "we get some time off to pack up whatever we want for the silo. We can order things, but who knows how long it'll take to get them."

"Are the other silos in Wyoming being manned next Thursday also?"

"That's my impression. All 18 in this area will have the four-person crew underground starting next Thursday. In fact, from what the colonel said, all 54 will be manned, with maintenance support up and functioning. Oh, we get crew uniforms and clothing issued to us. Our BMAT and MFT get Master Sergeant rank. I get lieutenant colonel, Susan gets major. It's really just a morale booster. We'll meet in the briefing room next Thursday at 1000 hours for a final briefing, then we'll be transported to the silo. No vehicles will remain out there for curious eyes. Until then, we'll do simulator rides together. It was nice meeting both of you."

Chapter 6: Somebody's Watching

Russian Army Sergeant Natasha Lebedev was scanning through routine satellite surveillance of the United States.

Sergeant Natasha Lebedev (photo taken in Sokolniki Park, Moscow).

This satellite, GK-12B, an all-weather reconnaissance satellite, routinely scanned across the middle and north parts of the US including northern Colorado, Utah, Wyoming, West Virginia, and northern California, taking photos which were downloaded to the central GRU reconnaissance database on a supercomputer buried three stories underground. In the event of WWIII, it was hoped that it would survive the initial salvo of incoming warheads and continue to be a backup for the mainframe located beneath a mountain range in Siberia. That mainframe managed the entire Russian air defense system, both manned and unmanned.

The sergeant was rather idly flipping through frames of Utah which looked pretty much the same from week to week, when up near Beaver, Utah, she noticed a long round black tanker truck. That alone got her attention. In the US, tanker trucks were usually aluminum. She flipped through the frames to verify what she suspected: it was parked. Somewhere, in some other photo, she had seen this truck before.

She typed into her mainframe access keyboard "MATCH TRUCK Photo 5893UT" and waited. It took several minutes but the screen eventually showed: "MATCH IS 8450CO." Next, she set up her screen to display two columns and typed "SHOW Photo 8450CO." And there it was: the identical-looking truck. She searched the code database for the other photo. It was taken a week ago four miles north of Cripple Creek, Colorado. She zoomed in on both trucks. They looked identical in every way. But what were they carrying and what were they doing on empty one-lane dirt roads? She looked for the DOT warning placard, only to discover the placard holder was empty. That was very odd. She could see no one around and no activity. Still, it was a mystery that needed to be solved. Americans sometimes behaved very oddly.

Natasha, clacking at the keyboard, searched for any vehicles on those two roads in the last 30 days. Her query revealed only two Forest Service patrol cars present on different days. There was nothing else except the truck. Next, she asked for an infrared scan within a 20-mile diameter of the location of the trucks. For this, she'd have to wait for the next satellite passes. Given how remote these locations were, the presence of more than a few people could merit further investigation. She logged off and went home to her family's apartment near the downtown market. A few shots of vodka, some bread and stew, then a dreamless sleep.

Two evenings later, at 1900 hours, she saw the requested infrared scans had been delivered to her inbox. She looked at the Utah scans first. These were taken at five-second intervals and showed heat from the front of the truck. This meant it was running or recently had been running. In the forest were several pairs of people. There was another heat source within a quarter mile of the truck, cooler than the people. For every pair of people, this heat source was present – square shaped, about 5' x 5'. She reset the computer's search range to 20 miles. Zooming in, she counted 18 of the square heat sources, most with no people present. She checked the times of the scans. All were around 2100 hours.

The Colorado scan showed the same patterns. There were 18 square heat sources and some people paired. *What would cause that distinct pattern? And what were the trucks carrying?*

Next, she zoomed in on the pairs of people. To her surprise, some appeared to be holding hands, two pairs appeared to be embracing, and several appeared to be sitting close to one another. She didn't understand any of this. Sighing, she took a sip of coffee from her favorite mug and tried to clear her mind. She thought back to her computer training classes and what her instructors had told her repeatedly: The right questions, coupled with the right search knowledge, could solve anything. So, what should she ask? She doodled on a pad: *18, 18, pairs of people, tanker truck. Possibilities?* She typed in the data she had, including the square heat sources, wondering if they could be from an exhaust. The computer began processing these entries as she waited, sipping on her coffee. A short time later, the computer displayed its findings: "US Titan II 70% probability."

She stared at the screen and thought for a minute. *What were the missing pieces?* She typed in "SEE 5893UT and 8450CO pattern of 18 square heat sources. FIND third similar pattern." The computer began its task. She went to refresh her coffee and when she returned, she typed in her user code and the screen displayed: "SEE 8931WY." This photo was taken the same night as the other two, in what appeared to be a remote area in Wyoming. The photo revealed several strip mines, in addition to 18 square heat sources. She could tell without zooming in that the heat sources were identical. She typed in all three infrared scans, along with "pairs of people," "54," and "tanker truck." The computer response was immediate: "Titan II 90% probability."

She stared at the screen in disbelief. An obsolete, liquid-fueled, long-range missile system deactivated in 1987. A system that carried the largest nuclear warhead ever in the US arsenal. The ramifications echoed in her mind. If the computer were right, it meant 54 hidden nuclear warheads were likely aimed at her country.

She took a blank form out of a tray and logged the search parameters and keywords. Under the heading "Results" she wrote, "Probability 90% of 54 hidden Titan II nuclear missiles." She sealed the report in an envelope and addressed it to Duty Officer, Missile Section. This was her first big discovery as a missile intelligence sergeant. Perhaps she'd get a promotion.

Upon receiving the report from Sgt. Lebedev, the missile duty officer, Gregor, wasted no time. He typed in the key words, and the screen showed the same result. He packed up the form from the sergeant and went down the hall to the office of the deputy director for missile intelligence, a colonel. After his secretary announced him, the duty officer silently handed the colonel the envelope. The colonel read the report and the duty officer's annotations.

"Gregor, it seems Missile Intelligence was more adept than we thought to spot this. Of course, the premier has known about these warheads for years. They're on the first strike target list. It would be best if knowledge of their existence didn't spread. It might upset the international balance of things: each country threatening to destroy another, but none doing so. We don't want to confuse the balance of nuclear weapons in the world."

"I understand."

"I hope so. I hope there will no further mention of this old, outdated system. It's hardly worth our notice but be assured, it's targeted. No mention of this by anyone, especially that sergeant probably blabbing around home about how her discovery might get her promoted and save the Motherland. She must never mention those old missiles. Do you understand?"

Gregor nodded. "I understand. It will be as you wish." He then stood and walked out of the office.

Deputy Director for Missile Intelligence (second from right). Photo taken in Apshi, Russia. (One of few known photos ever taken of the deputy.)

    Sergeant Lebedev didn't make it home that night, nor any other night. After a day passed with no news of her, neither her family nor work associates mentioned her again. Rather, she quickly became someone who never existed. Memories of her would fade over time, hastened by a little vodka. If some reminder such as a lost earring or keychain would bring her to mind, no words were ever spoken. In some societies, one learns how to behave and how to think in order to have a long and happy life.

Chapter 7: An Unsettling Meeting

The president of the United States noted on his appointment schedule a new meeting with the head of NASA, the national security advisor, the chairman of the joint chiefs, the counselor to the president, the secretary of defense, the White House chief of staff, and General James Clegg, chief of operations at NASS, Inc. He called his secretary.

"Julie, what's this meeting about that was added into the schedule today at 11 a.m. today? Looks like a lot of important people. Another budget problem? Some sort of scandal?"

"My money is on a scandal with this group. They wouldn't tell me what it was about," she replied.

The president went through his morning appointments. He was in a good mood that morning and hoped to maintain it. At 11 a.m., his secretary guided in the distinguished group and showed them to their seats around the presidential desk.

"Well, gentlemen, what brings so many important people to my office before lunch? General Clegg, nice to see you back in Washington again."

The general nodded in response. The president sat behind his desk and waited to see who the spokesperson would be. With this group, concerns were almost always related to budgets.

The head of NASA began. "Mr. President, I'll get right to the point. We have a problem of worldwide importance. An asteroid 10 miles long is projected to hit Earth or come close enough that the effects will practically be the same. At best, we're talking a miss in the low orbital range. It's a little early to tell, but this could be a hit somewhere north of the equator. This is the one we hoped would never happen."

The president listened carefully, sat back in his chair, and let out a long, deep breath. He looked around the table at the somber, rigid faces staring back at him, then turned to the head of NASA. "This could be the end of life on earth if we don't act fast. How big did you say it is? Ten miles?"

"Yes, sir. Ten miles long, five miles in diameter."

"Mankind has never encountered anything like this in all of recorded history," General Clegg said. "We need to utilize our planetary defenses."

"I agree," the chairman replied. "We should do everything we can to defend ourselves. But we don't have anything big enough to stop this."

The president looked incredulous. "Well, does this distinguished group have a recommendation?"

The head of the National Security Agency spoke up. "I recommend we say nothing publicly. Nothing can be done to stop something this big, and the news would cause worldwide panic. It's imperative this doesn't get out, and we can focus our efforts on rebuilding afterwards."

"Is rebuilding even possible?" the president asked. "Can we come back from this? Let me see the data."

The head of NASA put up a slide as he answered. "Size in this case matters, but not as much as velocity. And this one is headed directly towards us. The critical aspect here will be the energy delivered by the asteroid at impact. We believe the comet that wiped out the dinosaurs had a radius of about five miles and dispersed approximately 3×10^{33} GeV of energy within a local region in a matter of seconds. In layman's terms, that's about a thousand times more energy than what would be released in a full-scale nuclear exchange – delivered at a single impact point."

"Would all life on earth end?" the president asked.

"No, sir, but the country where the impact happens will likely be eradicated."

The Head of NASA handed out a data sheet which read: "Impact Velocity of this asteroid: 44.71 miles/second.

"Impact Angle: 45 degrees.

"Energy before atmospheric entry: 3.67 x 1024 Joules = 8.76 x 108 = 946.08 Megatons of TNT plus more, depending on variables.

"Crater Diameter: 219 km = 136 miles.

"Crater Depth: 1.5 km = 0.93 miles."

The president looked at everyone, his frustration evident. "So, are there other recommendations besides doing nothing? Do we need to run for shelter before impact? What about Cheyenne Mountain or the underground bunkers at the Greenbrier Hotel or Fort Meade? Can they survive this?"

"No, sir. No shelter can survive such an impact," the head of NSA replied. "At .93 miles, the crater depth alone will destroy any underground shelter. And that's a conservative estimate. All we can do is disperse the government and military. At the speed it's moving, we can only estimate the impact point within a few miles, and we won't know until seconds before it hits. Wherever it hits, that country will likely be destroyed."

The secretary of defense remarked, "All nations except China let civil defense slide away after the Cold War. But even China won't survive a direct hit on a city. Their shelters are steel but not deep enough to withstand the damage from a direct hit. Not only that, but the impact will throw up a cloud of dust that'll encircle the earth, causing nuclear winter. We're working with seismologists to determine how far away earthquakes might ensue. Those could wipe out dozens of cities not hit directly."

"Could this split open the Earth's crust?" the counselor to the president asked.

Everyone around the table looked blank, as no one knew exactly what an object this large hitting earth would do.

"Does anyone know whether this could knock the earth off its axis?" the president asked. "Could there be more asteroids heading toward us? What if multiple asteroids make impact? For all we know, there could be 20 of these heading towards Earth."

The president sat in silence for a minute, grim faces staring back at him. "I suppose we can't coordinate with the world's nuclear powers to re-target all of our 500 Minutemen III ICBMs, SLBMs, and all Russian, Chinese, French and English long-range missiles to break this thing up and deflect it?"

"Sorry, Mr. President. We don't have enough firepower in the world," the White House chief of staff answered. "At this point, I think all we can do is disperse the government to various underground locations and hope it hits somewhere else."

"We'll have to do any evacuations at night and use unmarked vehicles. No helicopters. We should start tonight, maybe with the cabinet secretaries," the counselor to the president said.

The president drummed his fingers on the tabletop. "How long do we have before impact? And does anyone have any other thoughts?"

"Seven," said the NASA director.

"Seven? Seven days? That's all we have to evacuate the government without the media getting wind of it? For fuck's sake!"

General Clegg raised his hand. "Sir, The chairman of the joint chiefs and I have a thought we'd like to discuss privately with you, given it's classified."

"Is this a really useful idea, General? It better be."

The general nodded. "It's a good, practical idea. Highly classified. Dark project status. Funded in secret. If we can have a minute of your time after the others leave, sir, you can judge for yourself."

The president sighed. "All right. I'll talk with the rest of you later and advise you on starting government evacuations late tonight. That's all for now." After the others had left the room, he turned to his remaining guests and offered some gallows humor. "How about a drink to toast the end of some random country? Help yourselves over at the bar."

General Clegg cleared his throat before speaking. "Mr. President, this may be somewhat unsettling, but the truth is we have a lot more nuclear power than we've let on in public, as perhaps do other countries. While it looks like we, alone, don't have enough megatonnage to stop this asteroid, if you combine what we have with Russia, China, England, and France, we can deflect the asteroid so that it misses us. The only question is will all nations use all of their long-range missile weapons to stop this thing from coming, or will they hold back and save some for leverage afterward? Or to start a war? This can't succeed unless all countries commit *all* their nuclear missiles, including any hidden ones."

"Okay. So, what's your plan, General?"

"Sir, we have some of the missiles we need available here in the US. If we can get China, Russia, France, and England to launch theirs – everything they have – that'll add to our firepower considerably. We could get Israel on board, too, but their warheads are all short-range or delivered by airplane. Not very useful for a situation like this. There is, however, a classified plan that could add enough bang to our armament to make a big enough difference to deflect this asteroid."

"Yes?"

"Sir, this plan is highly classified. Its use would bring discredit to the United States, your administration, and the entire western world if knowledge of this project were made public. It's critical this be kept under wraps."

"I'll do my best, General. You have my word. Now, what's the project?"

"Sir, Titan II was decommissioned between 1982 and 1987. We had 54 alert missiles with 9-mt warheads on them, plus other launch vehicles in storage as part of the space satellite launch program. Those 54 missiles were decommissioned, and the launch vehicles were used for space launches. Most of them were used in the Gemini program. One of the objectives of that program was to discover how people adapted to long-duration space flight. The original deployed warheads were stored."

"Okay, so the warheads are in storage, but the launch vehicles are gone. How does that help us? If we can't get those warheads off the ground, they're useless to us."

"We have the launch vehicles we need, sir."

A look of impatience came over the president's face. "You just said the launch vehicles were removed from the silos and used for space satellite launches."

"Those 54 were. They're gone. But we have another group at our disposal. Well-hidden."

"Hidden? How many are hidden? Titan was a huge complex. Are we talking about one or two? That's not going to help us much."

The general stood at attention to communicate the news. "There are 54, sir."

"What? What the hell are you saying? Are you telling me there are 54 long-range missiles hidden away here in America?"

"Yes, sir."

"Nuclear-armed, ICBMs?"

"Yes, sir."

"Fueled up?"

"Yes, sir. Liquid oxidizer and fuel. Two stage. Carrying fully functional 9-mt. nuclear warheads. Those are in addition to the stored warheads."

The president looked at him in disbelief, then picked up the phone. "Julie, I want no further interruptions, no appointments, until I say so." He then hung up the phone and sat back in his chair. "Let me make sure I understand this, General. You have 54 hidden Titan II liquid-fueled missiles that can launch. So, where are they? They're not on any alert I'm aware of. And all these missiles are armed. That's what you're telling me?"

"Yes, sir. They're each armed with 10 upgraded M-53 warheads, each with enhanced explosive capability. The Titan II originally carried only one warhead. Our contractors have upgraded each missile to 10. Not even our launch crews know about this. They still believe it's one, which is in our best interests. In total, sir, you have another 540 warheads at your disposal to meet this threat. Fifty-four missiles, each with 10 warheads. That'll pack one hell of a punch, Mr. President. The crews can decode a launch message, get the keys, run the launch checklist and have the engines ignite in less than three minutes. They're located in Utah, Wyoming, and Colorado. Part of a classified program managed by a company called NASS.

"Each missile is currently targeted against some global hot spot in case of trouble. Flight time to anywhere in the world is about 32 minutes. All of them can be retargeted in about an hour from a central information computer room. With the upgrade, they can be networked together to impact the same location at the same time, down to plus or minus 10 seconds."

The president looked out from the Oval Office window at the groundskeepers beautifying the lawn. It was a beautiful day outside. "Are the systems automated, General?" he asked.

"To the extent possible. Each missile can attack only one of three loaded targets, which means the warheads from each missile can't be divided between multiple targets. It's one target per missile, each with 10 warheads. All 10 warheads are set for either air or ground burst, and each missile is manned by an experienced launch crew of four people. At least half of each crew is ex-military, with prior ICBM experience. They know what they're doing."

The general sat as the president turned from the window to look at him. "Why was I never told about this project? What would the Russians and Chinese do if they knew there were another 540 live warheads that could be aimed at them? The implications could be enormous."

"I understand, sir," replied the chairman of the joint chiefs. "The project started back when Titan II was under construction. We built duplicate silos, warheads, maintenance tunnels – everything using non-specific funding or black ops funds. It was meant to be a Top Secret project and we've managed to keep it that way. Of men currently in uniform, I'm the only one remaining on active duty who knows of it."

"Who runs the program?"

"General Birmingham, sir. He's the president of NASS, Inc. General Clegg is a member of General Birmingham's team."

The president nodded. "Have you seen these missiles?"

"Only once, a year ago. My predecessor briefed me, and I'll brief my replacement when the time comes. No president has ever been informed of this, which allows for plausible deniability if the program were leaked or the press found out. The silos are well-hidden in remote areas, and they're not visible from the sky. All that shows is a small hunting cabin. Inside, there's an access stairway and elevator leading down to the silo. The silo door and main entrance steps are camouflaged, and there's an isolation cage for entry authentication. The launch crews stay in each silo for five years, and they're paid a considerable sum to keep quiet. Some civilians stay for years working on the systems. Nothing comes into the silos from topside except RVs, if needed. All supplies and maintenance are done from tunnels connecting the silos with maintenance and supply depots underground. There's nothing to photograph. It's basically a large underground network of tunnels. Launch crews can't access the tunnels without a retina scan and prior authorization. They're restricted to the silo's underground living area, the missile area, and the cabin on the surface."

"Well, they may not be noticed now, but they will be when they launch, General. Some satellite will spot them, and then the shit will hit the fan. Five-hundred-some missiles we never officially declared. The whole fucking world will be up our ass for going against nuclear treaties, and we'll never hear the end of it from Russia and China, assuming they don't flat-out attack us."

General Clegg locked eyes with the president. "With all due respect, sir, the shit's already about to hit the fan. But you can stop it and come out of this looking like a hero to the American people. And if Russia and China want to bitch at us for saving our country, let 'em bitch. They'd do the same thing in this situation if they had to, and we both know it."

There was a tense moment of silence.

"How fast is it moving?" the president asked.

"About 85,000 miles per hour, which means we don't have much time," the chairman replied. "We have to program the targets, and all nations on board with this have to hit the asteroid at the same time.

Reprogramming a target takes about an hour in Titan. It's not a last-minute task. If we're going to do this, we need to get going."

"Do Russia and China know about this asteroid?"

"They haven't said anything, but we think they probably know it's coming toward us. Their astronomy is as good as ours," the general replied.

"I'm sure they know," the chairman agreed.

"And the French and the English?"

"Probably the same. They probably know, too."

"Okay, then. I think the next move is to meet with the Chinese, Russian, English, and French ambassadors privately and tell them about the asteroid. See if they have any aces up their sleeve they'd be willing to share, though I doubt it. Gentlemen, I'll talk with you more later about this matter, but with six days left, we'd better meet with the world's nuclear powers ASAP. See if we can stop this thing from blowing us all to hell. Oh, and what about targeting? Who's responsible for that?"

"Right now, each is targeted by NASS against some global hot spot in case of trouble. A committee of retired officers does that. There's one retired CIA military officer who knows. He works in the anti-espionage directorate and has some Moscow agents who report to him. He checks to make sure other countries don't know about the hidden missiles. There may be a few civilian budget employees who know what they see in reports and budget requests, but they're not involved in the daily operation of the silos. Everyone else involved works for NASS."

"Are there other systems in this program that aren't ICBMs?"

"Yes, sir," the chairman replied. "Lots more. NASS only manages the Titan II program. There are plenty of other civilian companies running other weapons programs for supposedly deactivated weapons. My personal favorite is the battleship program."

"How many ships are in that program?"

"Eight, sir. New Jersey, Wisconsin, Missouri, Iowa, Alabama, Massachusetts, Texas, and North Carolina."

"So where are the crews?"

"They're on board, sir, ready to sail. Visitors never see them, or if they do, they believe they're part of a visiting group, perhaps at a private dinner."

"What the hell? You mean they live on board?"

"Yes, sir. Visitors assume the resupply and maintenance work they see is all just part of maintaining the ships. Much of that work is done in view of the public. Even fuel resupply. That's part of maintaining the museum ship, though that gets done at night. The crew stays proficient through simulators and computer interactive training that's amazingly real, especially the ship-handling simulations. With automation, we've been able to reduce the crew somewhat. It's currently 200 enlisted and 30 officers."

"And they're all on board now?"

"Yes, sir. Those ships are fully armed with cruise missiles; they can be out to sea in two hours. The crew members are permitted to go ashore since people might not believe them if they said they lived on the ship."

"I see. So, we have hundreds of Titan II missiles we can use to knock this thing off course, assuming everything goes as planned. What about our MX and Minuteman III missiles?"

"Right now, sir, all the remaining MX missiles and warheads are in storage," General Clegg replied. "But we can't fire a Minuteman and reload the silo right away. It takes months with those. Our best missile strength is Titan II. It's crewed and ready to go. Fifty-four hidden silos, mostly in remote, forested areas. Very well hidden. Built back when the silos known to the public were constructed – the ones outside Wichita, Little Rock, and Tucson. These hidden ones were listed in the budget as training and education facilities. They're all well-constructed. Sturdy and reliable. It's our best option by far."

The president looked out the window again. *What an amazing planet we live on,* he thought. *And now, one asteroid could destroy it all. We're gonna have to hit this thing with everything we've got.* He gathered his thoughts for a minute, then turned back to the general. "You said those missiles are nuclear armed. How fast do they launch?"

"Yes, sir. Nuclear armed, and they can launch within a minute at one of three possible targets. Switching targets can be done by pressing a button for target 1, 2, or 3. It's *loading* the targets that takes time. Crews are sent a message identifying which number to select. They don't know what the target is or where it's located. It takes about an hour to load a replacement for one of the targets with the older technology we're still working with. It's due to be upgraded soon, but it hasn't happened yet."

The president nodded. *Well, that's typical,* he thought. *Upgrades to government equipment* never *happen when they're supposed to.* "What about the crews, General? Wouldn't all that in-and-out traffic give them away?"

"Well, sir, like the battleship program, the Titan II crews live there. They don't come and go. They stay there. Five years in the silo and each volunteer gets a million dollars. The Titan crews are four people. Just recently we decided they can come up to ground level and walk around at night, but we've found they rarely bother. It does take some psychological training to be underground for five years with no contact with one's prior life, but the program has gone reasonably well. We developed a program to restore a lot of the youthfulness in our crewmembers."

"Yes, but five years in a missile silo, with only three other people around to keep you company…Wouldn't they come out of that unhealthy? What about relationships, interactions…*life?* How can four people stay down there that long and not go stir-crazy and end up killing each other? Are these mixed gender crews?"

"We solved the health issues and the issue of aging. Of course, that can never be made public, or we'll have overpopulation and mass starvation. In some ways, the project has reaped numerous medical advantages for the military and space programs. We also solved the challenge of motivating people to spend five years in relative isolation, with no interaction with the outside world."

"How'd you manage that?"

"Simple. Using medical technology and procedures far beyond anything known to the public, we make people young again and match them up with their one true love, whom we also make young. A combination of cloning and cell mutation and situational adaptations. We conduct thorough investigations to find people who were once couples and want to get back together again. People who've been pining for each other for decades. They want a second chance at life together, and that's what we give them. They both get a million dollars and 50 years of their life back. They get to live and work together for five years with another young couple, after which they can leave if they want. You'd be surprised how many couples stay even longer than that. And we get experienced, highly qualified people to man our missiles to defend America. It's a win-win.

"Rest assured, Mr. President, these people are carefully screened for the program, and work with the best therapists and hypnotists. Both parties must be willing. No one is forced to take part in the program. The age reduction is amazing, sir. We take 70-year-olds and make them 20 again. Modern medicine and therapy can do wonders if one has the proper budget."

The president said nothing for a minute as he took in the general's words. He briefly considered asking about the status of numerous other supposedly retired or decommissioned programs and operations, but thought better of it. Time was of the essence, and based on what he'd just been told about the Titan program, he suspected he already knew the answer. He also thought back on two very important words he'd heard that morning: *plausible deniability*. Sometimes it's good to know things. Other times, it's just as good to *not* know.

"So, gentlemen, we have 540 more warheads than we've been reporting all these years for the arms limitation talks with Russia. Do Russia or China know or suspect anything about these missiles?"

"No, Mr. President," the chairman replied. "We're confident they currently have no knowledge of this."

The president nodded. "Okay. Well, thank you, gentlemen, for a most unsettling meeting. I need to think on this a bit. I'll speak with both of you again very soon."

The general and the chairman left the oval office while the president paced around the room, thinking. He picked up the phone. "Julie, get me the directors of the FBI, NSA, and CIA on a conference call; be sure it's scrambled and coded, and call me back when you have them."

Ten minutes later, Julie said, "Mr. President, all three are on the line for you."

"Gentlemen, I won't keep you long, but I want each of you, working independently, to get me any information you have on a company called NASS doing business with the government on classified projects in Utah, Wyoming, and Colorado. It's imperative this investigation and your findings be kept secret. Consider everything highly classified. I want you to pick two people each to do this research for me. No vast groups of investigators running out west, and no press leaks. Nothing. Whoever you pick must keep this to themselves. No discussions with family or hints to the press. Use whatever government computers you wish under my authority. I'll have Julie send a letter over to you by courier.

"Now, here's the tough part. I need whatever you can find in 24 hours. See what they're buying and where it's being shipped. Look for large quantities of items. Check their payroll, too, and see if anything jumps out at you. That'll be all, gentlemen."

Five minutes later, the president was back on the phone. "Julie, get my wife on the phone wherever she is. I believe she's headed back here from the airport."

Shortly thereafter, the president's wife called from her motorcade, on her way from the airport after giving a speech that morning to the Freshwater Conservationists of Wisconsin.

"Sarah, this is Jim. I want you to do something, and don't ask why, and don't say anything in front of the kids. When you get back here, don't use a helper, but pack a suitcase for me, yourself, and one each for the kids, and just set them ready to go in the bedrooms. Don't ask why. Dress for a colder climate than here, okay? We may have to go somewhere."

He hung up a few seconds later, sighed, and poured himself the strongest drink he could find from the bar.

Chapter 8: Seduction in the Morgue

At CIA headquarters, the night duty officer for Russia was logging incoming messages. Such messages were often smuggled out of countries whose goals were contrary to the US government's goals, in hollow buttons or eye glasses, before eventually reaching an American embassy. From there, they were encrypted and sent to CIA headquarters via satellite. The duty officer wasn't interested in how the message reached the embassy or who originally composed it. By the time it arrived at CIA headquarters, it was about as interesting as an ad for copy paper. His only concern was that he routed incoming traffic to the correct office, even if there was no office destination in the message. After it was automatically decoded, this one from Cairo seemed a bit odd.

CAIRO01330813. FOR CIAUNK FROM: SNOWBIRD47 SGT NATASHA LEBEDEV MISSILE INTELLIGENCE RECON GRU HQ MISSING FROM WORK STOP APPEARED VERY EXCITED AT CLOSE OF WORK TUESDAY STOP

The night duty officer typed back to the embassy in Cairo:

SNOWBIRD47 STATE LOCATION. He was gratified to read the reply two minutes later. SNOWBIRD47 SLEEPING AMBASSADOR'S QUARTERS. GUARDED. EXTRICATE FOR INTERROGATION. DIPLOMATIC AIR.

The duty officer logged off and thought about the routing. He then routed the messages to the senior anti-espionage officer, who would read them in the morning.

Bryce Duncan was a CIA anti-espionage officer who had spent his entire military career viewing the enemy as a series of jumbled letters on his screen that could be un-jumbled if the correct cypher code were applied. Retired from active duty, he simply changed clothes and moved from the Pentagon to a different office at CIA headquarters in Virginia, but continued working in anti-espionage. He was reading the incoming traffic from the US embassy in Cairo. The third message was from SNOWBIRD47.

Bryce Duncan (DAD) at CIA headquarters in Virginia.

It was unusual that the originator was actually at an embassy because it meant a one-way trip. One could hardly reappear at a Russian job after an unexplained absence. He decided to investigate further before acting. He typed in a restricted access code, then SEE SNOWBIRD47.

SNOWBIRD47 (photo taken in Cairo at the American Embassy).

A photo of a young woman appeared. Recruited while at the University of London a few years ago. Few messages had ever arrived from her, and none of any importance. She wasn't exactly a sleeper agent, but one so low-level as to almost not be there. Sometimes people who aren't noticed are useful. Bryce thought for a minute. That she had messaged and left her personnel job at GRU headquarters (Russia's intelligence agency) to do so meant that to her, at least, someone's disappearance was very, very important. Thus, the first step was verification.

Bryce accessed a list of agents at GRU who might be able to obtain some information without appearing inquisitive. He came across the name "Alya Kuznetsov" and scanned her profile. Personnel recruiter for GRU headquarters, degree in computer programming, knowledge of sign language and shorthand, unmarried but socially active. Frequents underground night clubs. Plays guitar ballads.

Alya Kuznetsov (photo taken in St. Petersburg, Russia).

She was diagnosed by US experts as not being interested in commitment based on her social life and number of breakups. Evaluators described her as flighty, a partier, much smarter than appears, dedicated to world peace more than the ascendency of one nation. She'd never been assigned anything important by the CIA. That was about to change, though, as Bryce thought she was perfect for the job he had in mind.

He was going to send Alya a travel sales email which would have to be deciphered using a one-time matrix. It would be sent to her from Intourist, promoting travel on the Siberian Express to Lake Baikal. The message would appear to originate from the Intourist central computer and would be automatically logged as an outgoing email sent to her personal account. The originator would appear as an actual Intourist travel agent. The tipoff that this email was for her spy role was simple: it began with the word "special" in the first sentence.

"Are you special? Deserve more than you get? Try a vacation via the Siberian Express to Lake Baikal in a first-class compartment. All meals and bedding provided. Concierge. Train departs Moscow central station Mon, Wed, Fri. 1000 hrs. Moscow local time. Intourist can assign a roommate to share the cost of a compartment."

Deciphered, it read "ANY INFO DISAPPEARANCE NATASHA LEBEDEV GRU HQ MISSILE INTEL MOST USEFUL. DAD." That would be enough. He'd either receive something or not.

****

Having received Bryce's message and accepted the assignment, Alya was at the Moscow regional morgue a short time later. She had a plan to gain information about Natasha through use of deception. Natasha almost certainly was dead, and if her body had been found, she'd be here. It was unthinkable in Russia for someone to walk away from a decent-paying job on a whim. Alya planned to seduce the night morgue attendant under the guise of someone looking for the office of lost and found for deceased persons. Of course, most items were stolen before bodies were delivered to the morgue, but the situation provided a plausible excuse for visiting late in the evening.

The sole male attendant on the night shift, just there to receive and store bodies, was about 30, long hair in a ponytail, who didn't consider dead people as ever having been people at all, but rather as always having been dead. The appearance of a young and very curvy lady who seemed to have wandered in by error was a piece of fortune from heaven. Usually, the night shift was boring. Bodies typically were found at dawn, when the night's mayhem came to light, and by then he'd be home sleeping. He stared at her in her red pull-over sweater and offered her peach vodka, which she accepted. She'd been careful to eat before coming here so that she wouldn't pass out from drinking, and she tried to sip while he drained his glass repeatedly.

She urged him to talk about the dead and what they died from, focusing on unusual deaths. She knew she was on the right track when he said, "I've got a murder in here. Young girl. Shot in the back of the head. Been here about two days. No family, and no one has claimed her for burial. I wonder if they even know she's here. The police don't seem interested. If no one claims her in a week, she'll be cremated."

He took another sip while she pretended to (curling her hand around her glass to hide the level of vodka, which hadn't gone down much). "I've never seen the face of someone murdered. Could I see her?"

"I don't know. It's not usually done, letting visitors see a murdered person."

"Wouldn't her family have to see her? In order to identify her?"

"Well, yes. Of course."

"Maybe she's part of my family. I should probably have a peek."

He smiled and played along. "Okay, I'll show her to you. Maybe she was part of your family."

They went through the main storage area into a smaller room with eight storage compartments. He knew which compartment she occupied. He snapped open the latch and pulled out the tray on which the covered body had been placed.

"Ready?" he asked. She nodded.

He pulled the sheet down to the waist. Blue sweater, her head turned left.

"This is what murder looks like. Back of her head. Look here."

She saw a hole about a pencil in diameter, with very little blood.

"Why isn't there lots of blood?"

"A very cold night. The blood simply froze in her head, and it's very cold in here, as well."

She recognized the face from the employment forms. It was Natasha.

****

The next day at CIA headquarters, Bryce Duncan received a one-time cypher message from the American embassy in Moscow. Transferred through several drops and agents on its way to the embassy, it was brief, and clearly from Alya. It read: "MOS080700 CIADAD NATASHA EXECUTED SHOT REAR HEAD. MOSCOW REGIONAL MORGUE. BODY UNCLAIMED."

Well, well, Bryce thought. *Someone didn't like whatever it was she was so excited about. I wonder what it was…*

****

Sergeant Vera Petrova (photo taken in Kiev).

Natasha had been replaced by a new face: Sergeant Vera Petrova, recently transferred to headquarters from Kiev. All non-commissioned officers (NCOs) in the career field of imaging intelligence came through the same training, thus making it easy to replace any losses. All the career field manuals, procedures, and chains of command were identical in any imaging intelligence organization, so orientation time was remarkably low. By the second day on the job, Vera knew her range of options, what she was searching America for, and what her job meant to the Motherland.

She spent much of her second day on the job examining American military bases to get oriented, but she kept thinking about her predecessor. She'd heard rumors while moving into her military-owned apartment a few blocks from her duty station. It was free to her as an NCO, and while plain, was better than most Moscow apartments. And "free" included all utilities.

Chapter 9: The Combat Crew's Arrival

Wyoming. Silo 3-7.

By 11 a.m. Thursday, they were on a winding Wyoming road. The colonel was driving with the four of them in the middle and rear row of seats, their luggage stored behind them. After 40 minutes, they turned onto a dirt road through timber, and approached a tall, rocky hill. As they approached, a section of the hill slid to the side on rollers, allowing them to enter a tunnel.

"One of the clever little things we've done with Titan," the colonel remarked. "One of many, to be honest."

They drove through the tunnel awhile, then pulled up beside a steel door which also slid open.

"We're here," the colonel said. "Things will look familiar in a few feet. Grab your gear. Now we hoof it."

They went through the steel door, along a hallway, made a left turn, and came to something everyone recognized, either from experience or training: the first of four 7-ton blast doors sealed shut with huge hydraulic pins. To get into the control center, they had to pass through three of the doors.

"Lead the way, Robert," said the colonel.

Robert pressed the Unlock button on the wall and the pins retracted, freeing the door. He then pulled it open, and they walked through and stopped at the next door. They all knew that the systems were interlocked so that only one door could be unlocked at a time. Robert pushed the Lock button and Sandy unlocked the next door. They repeated the process a third time, with a door on their left.

When that door was pulled open, they could see down a short cable walkway into the control center. Things looked like they had years ago. Gray paint everywhere, the smell of hydraulic fluid, artificial air, the chatter of monitored radio traffic. It all came back in a rush, an essential part of the rejuvenation process. To Sandy, it all seemed surreal they were going to spend five years here, with visits topside to see if the real world was still there, in order to earn a million dollars. She suddenly had doubts. This old liquid-fueled system might well kill them all. One only had to breathe a few parts per million of either the fuel or oxidizer, and that was it. They'd die a horrible death, starting in the lungs.

Led by the colonel, who in honor of the day had worn his Army uniform, they walked into the Level 2 control center.

My God, Susan thought. *These silos actually launched long-range ICBMs? Everything looks obsolete and probably has been for years. How safe are these liquid-fueled things anyway? Weren't there accidents involving fuel or oxidizer at Little Rock and Wichita? They never discussed that in our training. Wasn't there another tragedy years earlier? I'll have to ask Robert about that.*

Level 2, Control Center with commander's console in center. TV area rear left. Stairs to the left. Blast door behind photographer. Wikipedia (public domain).

A crew of four civilian contractors was packing up for departure. "Everything's good to go, Colonel," their boss said. "Maintenance has teams standing by in case any repairs are needed. Otherwise, when you're ready, the command post should be notified when your crew takes over and the bird is on alert, ready to fly."

The colonel nodded. "Doug, does your crew know what the three targets are?"

"Yes, it was necessary. We had to do some coordinating with your targeting people back at your HQ. They were able to load the new targets by phone rather than drive out here, which is at least a major improvement to the original system."

"Okay, then you guys can go. This crew will take the complex."

After they had gone, the colonel addressed the four.

"Well, it's all yours. Let the CP know you have the silo. You should do the daily verification in the silo, report any needed maintenance to maintenance control. The number is on both the commander's and deputy commander's console, along with other vital numbers like the command post. We've added a couple things. A disguised topside camera and the viewing TV screen above the deputy's console. There's an instruction booklet but viewing is easy and the camera can rotate 360 degrees and scan up or down. It has zoom capability, too. We've also added a direct phone to command control. Just pick it up if you need to. Most of you will think of this as contacting the command post. In our operation, it's manned by command-and-control veterans."

"If you need to reach me, my number's in your phone list."

He shook hands with each of the four.

"Remember, that's a missile ready to launch out there, not a simulator. Make a mistake, and that fuel and oxidizer will kill you, even with those Chemox masks. The silo has an emergency crew escape hatch and ladder to the surface. Your food and drink that you order by phone is delivered daily, as is laundry service. No more foil pack meals. Levels 1 and 3 are as you remember them, although we've updated the bunk room. I think you'll like that. You get whatever kind of alcohol you want, but watch the drinking. You might need your wits. And, just in case, your individual .38 cal. sidearms are in the cabinet where they used to be, along with ammo. We left the cabinet unlocked. If you need any help, call the command center. It has armed civilian response teams in case of unfriendly visitors."

He turned and walked away, closing the blast doors behind him as he departed. His job with this crew was finished.

The four looked around, their faces filled with amazement. Not only had they been made young again, but the equipment in the silo looked in perfect shape, just obsolete.

Susan and Sandy looked at each other. "Wanna look upstairs?" Susan asked.

They walked up the steps to the upper level where the bunk room, kitchen, and latrine with shower were located. Susan pushed the bunk room door open. "Oh wow, look what they did for us."

Instead of eight single bunk beds, there were now two queen beds made up with green government-issue blankets and oversize pillows. The top comforter had the USAF emblem on it.

"Well, that was nice of the colonel and his team," Sandy said. "Just like what newlyweds would like. Our own place of romance."

"That activity seems a bit out of place here," Susan replied.

"Yes. It's just weird to see these nice big beds encased in government green concrete walls with huge springs attached. Sort of takes the romance out of things. I think loving someone down here may be a chore for the next five years."

****

After the visit by Gregor, the duty officer, the deputy director for missile intelligence had been thinking. That was sometimes a bad thing to do, as thinking inevitably led to worrying, which led to vodka, and his doctor had warned him about the danger of heavy drinking at his weight and age.

The deputy director knew the premier knew nothing about the 54 liquid-fueled missiles. This was because every time something occurred that might have caused the Premier to know, the deputy director, being an active CIA agent, made sure it was promptly taken care of. He sent in no reports, his code name just one on a list locked away in Bryce Duncan's office safe. He'd never met another CIA agent and probably never would. Recruited on the University of Iowa campus 20 years ago, he'd been asked to do one thing only, if he ever could: stop the Russian government from discovering the existence of some offensive weapons in the U.S. arsenal. Let any weapons that were hidden remain hidden.

He'd never know how successful he'd been or if it ever mattered in the balance of world power, but such things mattered to a freshman named Peggy Sue, to whom he'd been engaged. After she died in a skiing accident, he was willing to help attain world peace if he could. The girl who recruited him looked like a freshman herself, but was actually 10 years older, with much experience in mending broken hearts of senior boys. So, under the general topic of long-range missiles, he tore up certain reports while telling his Russian comrades that information had been sent up the chain of command to the premier when, in reality, it had been shredded and incinerated.

The deputy was worried because this marked the second exposure of those 54 obsolete missiles carrying the most powerful of American warheads. The first event had been two years ago when a young NCO had made sense of the 18 vented heat sources in Colorado. After noticing them, he'd watched road traffic for weeks until he began to predict when various trucks would travel those empty logging roads. The patterns were complex, but he eventually found one that could be predicted: a few days before Thanksgiving and Christmas, a white box truck stopped, hidden by trees, close to each of those 18 exhaust vents. By timing its average speed between stops, he could deduce that it had stopped for almost an identical amount of time during each stop. And every stop was obscured by downed and damaged trees. Like a natural garage.

He also paid special attention to bridges. When he was first observing the truck, it avoided single-lane bridges, taking longer routes around and using only two-lane bridges. But after half the stops were done and the truck weight lowered, the truck rolled over one-lane bridges. The military wouldn't transport televisions around. They'd be permanent. But food a few days before a holiday was a good probability. It took frozen turkeys 3 days to thaw and 6 hours to cook. Where would enough food for 54 crews come from? Probably a local warehouse or store who'd get the entire order ready for a military truck pickup.

At a local bar that night, he discussed with a friend what he suspected about those 18 heat vents. Finding the food supplier would give him the justification he needed to claim he'd found hidden missiles. Unfortunately, his friend was a KGB informant. One phone call for a reward was enough to ensure the NCO was not at work the following day. But the deputy knew this information couldn't be concealed forever. Maybe it was time to retire to the Ural Mountains and go fishing.

Sergeant Vera Petrova had also heard about the young NCO who had gone to the stag bar and was not seen again. *Something's rotten with the state of the GRU Headquarters.* She idly flipped through today's photographs of military installations while thinking. Two MI NCOs found something important enough to likely have gotten them killed. The paper trail was two years old on the first NCO, but Natasha's event was just last week. Where was she?

Vera figured there were lots of places to dump a body around Moscow, but there were also people prowling around in lots of places looking for firewood, food, some shelter, somewhere to sleep, or a good place for a tryst. And the bodies from the night's depredations would go to the regional morgue. *So,* she thought, *let's see if we're lucky today.*

She picked up the rotary government phone, and after checking the index of county listings, dialed the regional morgue receiving desk. The man who answered was the same one who'd shown Alya the body of Natasha.

"Receiving desk, Andrey. Can I help you?"

"Yes, this is Nadja Hope Gash at GRU HQ. Is the body of Natasha, the sergeant from GRU HQ, still there?"

"No, I regret to tell you that military intelligence ordered the cremation yesterday."

"Is that unusual?" She decided to push. "Wasn't that an unsolved murder? There was no investigation?"

He hesitated to answer. Murders were never discussed by phone, if at all.

"There were unusual circumstances. We were only following orders."

"Whose orders?"

"I'm sorry. I don't remember. It was a colonel with an advanced title. Deputy director of something."

"Can you describe him? I'd like to cross check our standing orders in such cases with him to see if we're lacking correct procedures in our regulations in my division. We always try to do things correctly."

"I'm sorry, the order was read to us by a sergeant. The colonel was not here in person."

"You'd better hope that colonel really exists."

She hung up. There was nothing to be gained by having him try to identify her.

So, cremated with no investigation. No family involved. Did a colonel really order this with no written forms? That's most unusual. It speaks of someone with high rank. Someone used to power who wanted no evidence around. But why? To cover his tracks? Maybe he was involved? But again, why? *What did she find valuable enough to get her killed? And apparently while doing her routine job of looking at photos of American installations.*

She was flipping through yesterday's photos of American military bases in a swath across the middle of America. She filled out forms for a few convoy movements which looked routine, some of them to Minuteman III missile silos, some – the ones protected by helicopters – no doubt nuclear warhead convoys. Camouflaged tents always hid groundwork on Minuteman from spy satellites, but sometimes the task could be determined from the type and number of support vehicles at a particular silo. She wondered if she could deduce a missile support convoy from the vehicle composition. It seemed like a lot of loose pieces to manage. Yet those other two NCOs had found something important enough to get them killed by an important someone, probably an officer. Probably an officer in her chain of command.

Let's say there is such a traitor. She took out an educational plastic card with everyone's rank and title in her chain of command and started with those of lieutenant colonel rank and above. There were a lot of them in charge of various offices, but not so many in a direct line up to the premier. She looked through more boring photos of American military assets while she thought. *Everyone has a past, and traitors became traitors in the past. So let's try to discover who the traitor might be from where they were assigned in the past. In order to be a high-ranking traitor, one would have be turned when they were young. High-ranking officers didn't endanger their luxuries by becoming traitors after achieving their ranks. Maybe 15 to 25 years before.* So where had high-ranking officers in her chain of command been where they could act against the good of the Motherland an average of 20 years later? Almost always, the catalyst was love or ideology. Someone in love or someone personally hurt by an aspect of communism, such as family members being sent to jail or Siberia. She knew what she was looking for, but how to find it would require some thought.

She was scanning around central Colorado when she spotted multiple vehicles in camouflage paint with troops spreading netting over them. It was just a roll of the dice that the satellite took a photo just before they would've been hidden. Piles of branches, possibly hollow like garages, were gathered in a circle with one tree on its side. She took an eyepiece magnifying lens and looked closely at the tree. She thought she could see tires beneath the branches.

She sat looking at the tree, then looking away at a distant point, then back. This was an old WWI trick used by reconnaissance personnel to see details of the trenches from camera photos taken from two-seater airplanes. She tried to clear her mind and just look at the tree on the ground, then look at a distant point. Suddenly, she understood. It was a long crane lying on its trailer, with branches on top. Long enough to move an RV. She looked carefully at the road leading to the crane and did some measuring. She found a circle of debris the right circumference for a movable, camouflaged clam shell that would cover a security helicopter. RVs almost never traveled without an armed helicopter escort, and this one was the correct size for Huey rotor blades at 48' 3". She could also pick out troops with foliage on their helmets, and she noted their boots weren't disguised.

She meticulously filled in a report form documenting her evidence and conclusions. Again, she believed she had found the area of the 54 hidden missiles. Individual silos were marked by the 54 heat vents. She dropped the reporting form in the tray for the missile intel duty officer, Gregor, who read it with increasing anger. The Americans had 54 hidden heavyweight missiles left over from the Cold War. The proof was right here. He made some brief annotations and went off to see the deputy director for missile intelligence again. This time, he had absolute proof.

"What is it, Gregor? I have loads of paperwork to do. You keep popping in and out like a cuckoo clock in Berlin. What do you want this time? I'm busy as hell."

"Look, Colonel. Here's another report about those hidden missiles. But this time we know the location more accurately, plus one of our satellites apparently photographed a convoy delivering a warhead to an unidentified silo."

The colonel carefully read the report and examined the photos. "Yes," he mused. "It looks like some sort of convoy, but this appears to be tree-cutting equipment. Is this what you bothered me for?"

"Yes, Colonel, but look what happens when I had our computer section take what little we can see of what's beneath the top equipment and tree limbs. It extrapolated the extension of the lines, deleted shadows, then put it in correct ratio for size based on the trailer and tractor size for these convoys. Then, using the new AirClear brand machine we bought from the British through one of our sub-contractors, we created a 3D drawing of it sitting clearly on the flatbed trailer. Here it is."

The deputy was openly shocked. The drawing clearly showed a Mark 6 reentry vehicle which would contain a W-53 warhead. He bluffed for a minute, pretending to check the drawing against a USAF reference book. It was an exact match. It's range riding on Titan II exceeded 8,700 miles and could detonate anywhere in Russia. He wondered if someone had copied the drawing to expose him, but didn't think so. *School in America was a long time ago.*

This time, the deputy could not cover up the extent of the Titan discovery.

"All right, Gregor. I'll take it to the MI command outside of Moscow. A nice letter of commendation is headed to your personnel files. Maybe you'll earn a bonus."

The deputy went out to lunch, taking his car. In a large lot under construction, across the street from a park dedicated to the sacrifices of WWII, he assembled the emergency cipher machine from dashboard parts and his metal lunch box. He was badly out of practice with the cipher machine, but it was imperative to get a warning out before armed Russian interference could arrive at one of those 54 silos. The cipher machine was simple. It manually switched text into coded text which could be decoded at the receiving end, if one had the key. It wasn't particularly sophisticated, but useful in an emergency in a location where one didn't want to risk a radio transmission. Moscow was overlaid with monitoring devices that could easily trace a radio signal back to the deputy, whose code name was TUNA.

He then sprayed the paper with some special cologne that would cause it to melt in one hour unless sprayed with a process-halting antidote, then ripped it to pieces. The pieces could be sprayed with the antidote, then reassembled using a microscope. If he were caught with those pieces of paper before they melted, it would be very bad for him.

He walked across the street into the park, throwing crumbs to a group of pigeons. One, with a black stripe on its wings, rested away from the others. It was a homing pigeon who came to the park daily at lunch time to look for the deputy who called its name – "Honor" – and threw it a large piece of bread with the shredded paper inside. Without eating them, Honor flew the piece to the US embassy, just as pigeons had flown battle information in WWI. (If it had eaten the bread, the message still could've been recovered. Doing so, however, would've meant a *very* unpleasant fate for Honor.) When reassembled and transmitted to CIA headquarters via satellite and deciphered, it read:

"MOS092100TUNA TO CIAHQDAD. TROUBLE. HIDDEN LGM25CS DISCOVERED BY MI."

He next went to see the director and pass along the Titan discovery news. The director then went to see the premier, who thought it best to act immediately.

Krymsk air base in western Russia, with an 8,104-foot concrete runway, is the departure base for the combat-experienced Russian 7th Guards Mountain Air Assault Division, whose motto is "Courage, Valor, Honor." This unit had considerable battle experience including WWII, Hungary, First Chechen War, Second Chechen War, and the Dagestan War. Their flight configuration depends upon the mission, but they are parachute-qualified with mechanization as needed. One of their transports is the An-12, which can be reconfigured for in-air refueling. In March 1970 training, 240 of these workhorse planes dropped 8,000 troops in 22 minutes. It is one of the best multi-purpose Russian planes.

For this trip, they would be lightly configured with six crew including spare pilots, an EWO, a maintenance expert, 12 paratroopers, and four Tigr 4-wheel all-terrain troop carriers with a 687-mile range and paved road speed of 87 mph. Equipped with grenade launchers and machine guns, they could be dropped by parachute.

The commander of the 7th, Colonel Alekseev, consulted with the premier about the mission. The goal was to parachute in the vehicles and troops to take over one Wyoming silo and detonate the fuel and oxidizer underground transfer system, which would back flash through all the underground fuel and oxidizer piping, thus destroying all 54 silos. That system weakness had been overlooked when the silos were configured for loading and unloading of fuel and oxidizer through underground pipes and large hoses versus the truck-hauled trailers and hoses used during the Cold War.

The attack plan, as worked out by Plans and Programs Directorate and the Russian Army Research Laboratory, was to fly in along the Canadian and U.S. border at low levels. The team would then parachute at night into a clear field several miles from the silo. After the crew members were eliminated and the silos destroyed (security was not exactly tight in the civilian-manned silos since they officially didn't exist), the team would motor to the former Casper Army Airfield (1942 to 1945) which had two active runways, 03/21 at 10,165 feet, and 08/26 at 8,679 feet. During WWII, however, there were four runways for bomber practice. The two abandoned runways were still there and usable for an An-12 airplane modified with rough terrain landing gear. The airport was closed from midnight to 4 a.m. daily, with no manned control tower or radar. With the vehicles repainted with American markings, it would be possible to drive the 153 miles in the dark as an American military convoy, from silo 3-7 to Casper, drive the vehicles and troops onto the plane, and depart low-level using the abandoned WWII runway.

Preparations started with as few people knowing the real mission as possible. The pilots could get some practice landing time in a flight simulator. The actual landing would have to be on an unlit runway at night, but crews were trained in such procedures. The runway would be checked for debris by a local guide hired for that purpose.

Amanda had devoted a lot of thought to the Russian attack scenario, and she finally called General Birmingham at his home in Virginia on a government scrambled line. She chose Synthetic Voice #8 as the most reassuring to the general.

Chapter 10: Hidden No More

The next morning, Bryce at the CIA received a message from the deputy director: "MOS092100TUNA TO CIAHQDAD. TROUBLE. HIDDEN LGM25CS DISCOVERED BY MI."

He, too, was dismayed the hidden silos had been discovered. A program years in the making was about to be useless. He thought about what to do. He had no idea, but he knew the Russians would react with force against those silos. Probably localized attacks using paratroopers. He also knew the manner in which the program was being run was illegal.

In his wall safe, there was a red and yellow striped card in a plastic seal he'd been given years ago by the computer team. On the front, it said, "In any case when you have indecision, Open and Follow Instructions."

He snapped the card open. Inside were three lines of type: "CALL AMANDA, 800-USA-WINS, BETTER DEAD THAN RED." He used a scrambled line and called.

"This is your Amanda. I know who you are. I hope you are having a nice day," she answered.

"Screw you. I've heard about you. Miss Wonderpants who's going to save America. Well, listen to this news. Our 54 hidden Titan II missiles have been detected by Russian missile intelligence. What the hell do I do now? We're all screwed. Everything we've done in this program is illegal. Warheads, budget, the rejuvenation program, loads of felony charges…all our asses are going to end up in federal prison for years."

"Please wait. I am thinking. I will play some music to soothe you. You seem to have a high heart rate and indications of anger. Do not have a stroke or cardiac arrest. Do not hang up or go away."

He waited. Caribbean music played. He eventually found himself humming to the music and, upon realizing this, became even more agitated. He tried to stifle himself and be calm. His hand was twitching involuntarily on his desk.

After several minutes, Amanda said. "An armed response team sent by Russia is a 90% probability, using Russian paratroopers. Targeting probably begins with any northern silo. There will be no official statements from either Russia or America regarding that team regardless of outcome. A Russian aircraft could be part of a farm fair expo show in Cheyenne next week, or it might land elsewhere. I will take care of everything. Do not call me back. Do nothing yourself." The connection ended.

Amanda then sent a preemptive, coded message appearing to originate from Dad to the Russian Deputy Director for Missile Intelligence: "US101500DAD TO MOS101501TUNA. NOTIFY DAD AND AMANDA IF UNUSUAL RUSSIANS COMING TO AMERICA."

****

Robert was sitting topside in a folding beach chair when Susan emerged from the ground-level entrance door and dropped into a chair next to him.

"Well, here you are. Thinking great thoughts?"

"No, just mulling over some things about this project. We don't know if or how we're being monitored. We don't know if there's a real warhead on our missile. We don't even know if the other 53 silos are really active. We don't know if we call them by radio that we're even talking to them or someone else. Frankly, we don't know anything ourselves. The only information we have came from the colonel. He was the only source."

"We can find out one thing. Are our salaries going directly into our accounts we each set up? Like a direct deposit? A few phone calls could verify that."

Robert smiled halfheartedly. "What if we're not talking to the bank, but someone else?"

"I don't know. All I know is it's gonna be hard to cash a paycheck around here."

"This has all the makings of how do we ever know what's real? If we get a launch order and the 6-digit code opens the butterfly valve to mix the fuel and oxidizer to ignite the engines, how do we know who's ordering the launch? Surely not Tony. Too low ranking. So, *who*, then? And what are our possible targets?"

"We can't check where our missile's really going. It could be anywhere. NATO allies, somewhere in the US…We just don't know."

They sat in silence awhile, looking at the mountains scarred from strip mining.

"What about the warhead? Could we verify that it's real?"

"Maybe. We could take the classified tech order out to the silo, open an access panel, and see if it looks real, or is there nothing inside the covering? Even if it looks real, we don't have the expertise to know if it's nuclear or just high explosive. But that's the best we can do."

"How about the tools in the emergency war order kit? Anything we could use?"

"Maybe a Geiger Counter. It's in there for post war use to determine if it's safe outside. We might be able to get some readings inside the cover panel."

"Okay, let's get Jeff and Sandy and see who wants to go out there. None of us knows anything about a nuclear warhead."

After a group discussion, the crew decided the enlisted backgrounds would be best for examining any piece of the missile. The four of them sat in a circle on Level 2 of the control center. Robert began the discussion.

"I think Susan told you both what we hope to discover: Do we have a real nuclear warhead on our missile, or a fake one? Since none of us has had any training in nuclear warheads, we'll just have to do our best. If it's real, we especially don't want to mess anything up. Opinions?"

Sandy looked concerned. "Is it possible this could expose us to radiation?"

"I don't think so. Everything should be shielded in case minor maintenance is needed." Jeff and Sandy nodded as Robert continued. "Okay, you two. If you're up for it, get some tools and open the warhead access panel, then get on the radio net. We'll be listening here in the control center. Let's see what we're dealing with."

A few minutes later, Robert and Susan heard Jeff and Sandy each call in. "Team 1, how do you read?"

"Loud and clear."

"We're lowering work platforms now."

There was a pause while the Level 1 work platforms were lowered by hydraulics.

"Entering Launch Duct now."

"The warhead access panel is held on by four slotted screws. We're going to remove the panel now."

Several minutes passed while the team laid out drop cloths and removed the panel.

"Oh, no," said Jeff. "You're not gonna believe this. There's nothing in here. Nada. Zip. Empty. Just the nose cone. No high explosive, no big bomb…*nothing*. Like we're not even in the game. Just an expendable decoy, perhaps. There's no weapon at all here."

"Maybe that's it," Robert replied. "We're a decoy to make the enemy expend ordnance on us instead of on a real bird. Maybe we're an expendable decoy, but still have a role to play during the next global war."

"Maybe," Jeff and Sandy answered, sounding less convinced.

"Okay, team. Button up that access panel and come on back here. It's time to run the weekly power transfer test and let that old diesel run a bit."

Robert turned to Susan. "That warhead is supposed to weigh 8,800 pounds. Without anything inside, it probably weighs less than half that. I wonder how that changes the guidance requirements."

"Does it really matter? Our orders are to launch it, either way. It must have some role to play," Susan replied.

"I guess we don't get to know. But at least we know what we're launching. Or *not* launching, in this case. It's just a big shiny Roman candle. Happy 4th of July."

****

Roger Midgley, the president's special advisor for military policy, was on the phone to the Titan II targeting teams in Utah, Colorado, and Wyoming. He'd sent each team a set of mathematical navigation projections for the future position of the asteroid. His plan was to have all 18 missiles of each of the three-unit groups hit the asteroid together. The final group would attack using proximity fuses rather than groundbursts since, after 360+ explosions, there'd be only pieces of the asteroid remaining if the plan were successful. The final goal, of course, was to change the asteroid's course so it would miss Earth, or render the remaining pieces so small that they'd burn up harmlessly in the atmosphere.

Each of the three groups understood the task and was getting underway. Some missiles had been decoys; those missiles would receive a genuine warhead. All 54 of the hidden Titans would be targeted against this asteroid barreling toward Earth.

****

Vera had the freedom to look at photographs taken anywhere in America to detect enemy actions and search her assigned path across the country. The other photography missile intelligence NCOs were involved in the same task, but no one knew what the other NCOs were looking at. It was possible they were looking at the same location, but this increased the probability of verification if two independent people reported the same event and came to the same conclusions.

Vera's area was primarily a swath across the middle of the US, from Maryland to Colorado, Wyoming, and Utah to northern California.

What would cause an NCO in Missile Intelligence to become very excited?

Finding missiles.

What type of missiles?

ICBMs. The city-buster types that kill people of the Motherland.

What model?

She had to think about this, as there were three choices: newly developed, hidden current types, or hidden older missiles. She looked at her list. Choice 1 meant testing, movement, lots of people involved, lots of moving parts. Those moving parts included construction, supply, transport, manning, research, and testing. The manning involved lots of people moving around. Could she connect the dots?

Choice 2 involved hidden current types. Again, this meant people involved, transport, logistics, supplies, and preparation from years ago. ?

Choice 3, the hidden older missiles with nuclear warheads, probably large ones, meant some deception years ago that went unnoticed due to lack of good observation. This choice seemed most likely, though none could be counted out.

Vera put her list down and cleared her mind as she scanned photos of airbases in the Washington, DC area. What had she learned about Americans when she attended military high school? They were cowboys, gunslingers, shoot-from-the-hip people whose president lived in worlds of plausible deniability. Deny this, deny that, deny everything. For new weapon systems, the cat would be out of the bag anyway, at least eventually. That left hidden current types and hidden older types. Which one was likely to have escaped detection because satellite monitoring wasn't as good decades ago? Old types, of course. *There are old types and bold types, but no old bold types.*

She was looking for shy, hidden older types.

How old?

Atlas, Titan I, Titan II, Minuteman I, Minuteman II.

Which was earlier than good satellite images? Which had the largest warhead ever on a missile? Which had a rapid launch time?

Question 1: Atlas, Titan 1, Titan 2.

Question 2: Titan 2, 9 mt.

Question 3: Titan 2, Minuteman 1, Minuteman 2.

Only one system answered all three questions: Titan 2. Hidden, of course – probably across the middle of the US. Probably hidden when they were first deployed and kept operational even while 54 were deactivated. She recalled her MI school lessons. Stages 1 and 2 were used for satellite and manned space mission launches. Titan 2 was used in the space program, besides serving as an ICBM. It powered 12 Gemini launches, all successful. Two were unmanned (1964) and 10 were manned, flown 1965 and 1966 in preparation for the moon landing that many people in the US believed to have been faked by the government.

So, if hidden when first deployed, then 54 additional silos were needed, assuming the hidden number equaled the publicly known totals. And because Americans tended to like symmetrical designs, probably 18 in three locations. Say 12 acres each for 216 acres needed for 18 missiles. Separating them by at least 7 miles as was originally planned may not have been possible for the hidden ones, depending on terrain.

She doodled on her notepad while looking at photos of Offutt AFB in Nebraska. *Look for man-made patterns not within 10 miles of a town...Look for some sort of supply trucks...Look for crew vehicles...Look for military trucks where there are no military installations. How did those two NCOs find the missiles if not specifically searching for them?*

Trucks. Supplies, people, parts, maintenance. Support bases not too far away. They probably found whatever by accident. That means the hidden missiles are within my assigned territory. Away from a city. Probably in an area where few people go. Hot? Mountains surrounding the silos? Trees?

She thought back to the Cuban Missile crisis and the photographs that showed clearly what the Russians had been doing in Cuba. Trucks here and there, missiles everywhere. She clearly remembered watching a film of the US president speaking to the nation and pointing to those photographs.

Trucks and missiles. No people. Trucks and missiles. They had been only medium range, not the pure long-range ICBM. But they were long enough to see. She remembered the classroom lesson. Rudolph

Anderson Jr. was shot down October 26, 1963, in a U-2 reconnaissance plane while over Cuba. He was the only fatality of the Cuban Missile Crisis.

She suddenly had an idea. She'd try to trace Natasha's keystrokes, each of which was permanently recorded. In order to be able to collaborate, all the missile intelligence NCOs could access each other's keystroke logs.

She typed in "LOGNATASHA1GRUHQ0-144," which meant jump back 144 hours from now and come back to present time. After a minute of processing, the computer displayed: "REQUESTED LOG RESTRICTED TO ALPHA ACCESS."

She did not have Alpha access, even with her special clearance. Not only did she not have the log, but now someone could see she'd looked for it. She only asked once, hoping her request would be accompanied by other hundreds of routine requests for logs. So, that was that, unless she just happened upon whatever it was that Natasha had found. She continued looking at Nebraska.

Vera had spent some time wondering how to identify the GRU traitor and had narrowed the possibilities to three people: the director for missile intelligence, the deputy director, or the missile staff duty officer (SDO), a rotating position. To identify the SDO, she'd need to cross-check the name of the person on duty against what had happened that day. She suspected the situation could also be that something hadn't happened that *should* have, such as a discovery that wasn't acted upon. She had limited knowledge about intelligence discoveries that produced no reaction from the chain of command. All she could examine were her own reports and their effects.

She figured the probability was greater that the culprit was either the deputy or the director. If they were working for the CIA, they'd almost certainly have been recruited many years ago, probably in America. So, which had been to America for some length of time?

She read their official Russian biographies and discovered both had attended school in America to obtain their four-year degrees and improve their English skills, no doubt. The MI director attended the University of Texas, while the MI deputy received his degree from the University of Iowa. She assumed they completed their degrees in the normal amount of time. On the internet, she followed some trails of articles and was able to determine their majors: political science for the director and English for the deputy. Which was more likely to be influenced by Western ideals?

At this point, Vera was unsure how to proceed. She considered talking with both individuals under some made-up pretext to see if this led to anything revealing. She thought, though, that direct discussion might put the culprit on alert while resulting in no new information. *Hmmm. How does one discover anything about a person's school years without knowing who their classmates were?*

What sort of trails does one leave behind while attending college for nearly half a decade? The possibilities practically endless. Acquaintances, photographs, souvenirs, courses completed, teachers who might remember them, books checked out from the library. Who might recruit a new agent? It could be anyone. Male, female, young, old, teacher, student. It was impossible to tell, and good agents blended in well. An agent recruited years ago might be needed just once or twice in a lifetime, and were usually successful if matched well to the assigned task. Where to start was a critical question.

Vera suspected one avenue that might prove fruitful was yearbooks. In order to hide her interest, she planned to order yearbooks from different schools. The two she wanted, however, was the *Cactus* yearbook from the University of Texas, and the *Hawkeye* yearbook from the University of Iowa. The official biographies distributed to all members of the missile intelligence division would provide the approximate years. If one of them appeared in, say, the sophomore class photos in a certain year, then she would know the approximate graduation year issue. Seniors often had the most information about themselves in the graduation yearbook.

On the other hand, if an individual skipped the photo for the senior yearbook, it could be a clue that a serious negative event had occurred in prior years at that school. By buying the yearbooks across all four years of attendance, she might discover clues to what happened and how the culprit had been turned.

When the yearbooks arrived, including the distractor books from The University of Colorado, Wyoming, and Massachusetts, she first sought out the senior issue for both men. Then, she performed a tedious, painstaking examination of each issue. She knew that activity and club information was provided by students themselves, and could therefore be embellished or unreliable. The same could be true for entries listing future jobs, slogans, favorites, etc. In addition, every yearbook contained informal photos of groups, sports, and activities, often on pages located away from the formal poses. Those, Vera thought, might also prove useful.

She started with the missile intelligence director. Under activities, it showed band 1, 2, 3, 4; political science club 1, 3; psychology club 2, 3; Goodwill volunteer 1, 3; Future Farmers of America 1, 2; young politicians club 4; tutoring club 3. Intriguingly, it showed a clear pattern of fewer activities during his senior year versus his freshman year. Was that important?

She started the same way with the deputy director. Pep squad 1, 2; choir 1, 2; investment club 1; German club 2; exploration club 2; Food Service Advisory Board 3; For the deputy, there were no extracurricular activities listed during his senior year. None. His name was listed under "other graduates," with no photo. What would cause someone to skip their senior photo? A schedule conflict? Out of town at the time? Disinterest? Overall, there was little to learn from his senior class yearbook entry. That meant a long search for both individuals' photos in organizations, activities, and clubs sections of both yearbooks. Since some of the photos were top half of the face only, it also meant increasing the size of any posed photos and trying to match the top half of the face. With a good facial identification program and all photos interest already scanned, it wouldn't take long to match any identical photos to each other. *Not* having such a computer accessible to her, however, meant a considerable investment of time. Even then, there was no guarantee she'd recognize a match without the aid of a computer. It could perform this task in a fraction of the time with far more reliable results. Realizing this, Vera let out a long, deep sigh; like it or not, a manual search would have to be done.

She knew she couldn't rush the photo search. At the same time, she was anxious for results or at least some indicator of whom the turncoat was. She'd considered other ways of identifying him, including travel, buying habits, and food preferences. Yet she couldn't see any real way of moving forward other than what she was doing now.

Pouring herself some coffee, she sat in her living room and waded through the junior yearbook for the deputy. Page after page there was nothing. After several hours, she took a break. There was no easy way to speed up the search unless, rather than looking at most pages, she searched by page title. This was likely to miss some photo matches, but she decided it was worth it. Otherwise, she'd be an old lady by the time she finished searching. She looked at the index and corresponding photos, paying special attention to organizations included in his formal activity list in the yearbook. She tried his clubs and activities photos, finding him sometimes identified in a group photo. But there was no matching photo from which she could glean any information.

She was examining both of their sophomore yearbooks when she saw a possibility. Under the heading "New Loves," there was a female student sitting on the trunk of a car, her head in front of a male student sitting beside her. Only the top half of the male's face was visible, including his eyes and ears. His hands were on top of hers, palms down, resting on hers, which were palms up. Vera took her magnifying glass and looked at a posed photo, comparing it to the informal one. It looked like the same person. She looked at the young lady's photo, then searched through the small, formal class photos of the freshman and sophomore classes. This consisted of hundreds of different photos, but at least these were full-face format.

The one match for the deputy she thought she'd found was his formal sophomore class photo and the informal photo under "New Loves." With patience, diligence, and her magnifying glass, she found a match for the young lady in the freshman class, one year behind him.

Even better, in examining another photo of him during his very early flying days, she saw what appeared to be a gold ring on his left pinky finger. *That could be a girl's ring cut too small to fit on any finger besides his pinky,* she thought. It appeared to have numbers on the top, though the photo was too poor in quality for her to make them out clearly. Perhaps her graduation year? Or birth year? It looked very much to Vera like a graduation year cut. His senior graduation yearbook showed couples, but not the deputy and the young lady together, as they were in the other yearbook.

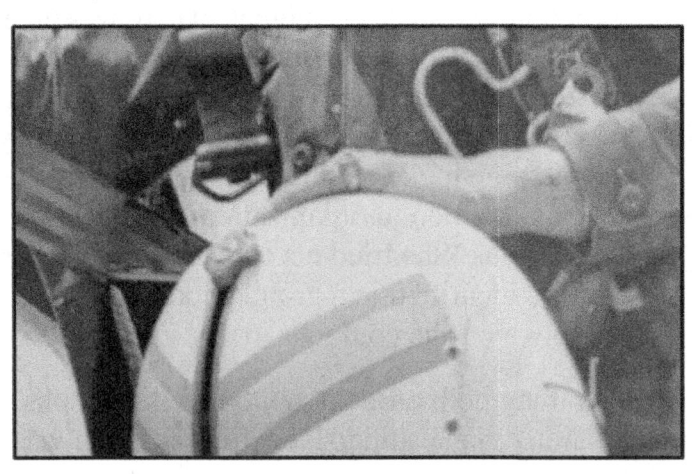

A woman's ring on the pinkie finger of the deputy director for missile intelligence(?).

With a vindicated smile, she remembered what the attendant at the morgue had said when asked who the colonel was who'd ordered the cremation of Natasha. He'd replied: "I'm sorry, I do not remember, but it was a colonel with an advanced title. Deputy director of something."

Deputy Director for Missile Intelligence, she thought. *And now I know something worth money, and perhaps a better life.* She stored her knowledge like bullion in a vault, ready to be used when needed.

Chapter 11: The Shell Game

Wyoming. Silo 3-7.

A loud warble sounded from the speakers on the command and communications consoles. Robert and Susan grabbed black crayons and individual markerboards, and copied the coded message.

TANGO 1, 5, 6, 5, 4, 2 SIERRA FOXTROT, VICTOR, ALPHA, TANGO, 5, 6 GOLF, SIERRA, MIKE, FOXTROT, CHARLIE, SIERRA, LIMA, DELTA, SIERRA, TANGO 5, 6, BRAVO, ALPHA, FOXTROT. I SAY AGAIN…

They double checked they'd copied the message correctly, then Susan pressed the ACK button on the communications console. She then opened the safe and took out the two decode pads. The message deciphered as follows: "SQ 3, SILOS 4, 7, 9, 15, 16 PREPARE FOR RV CHANGE OUT."

"Well, well," said Robert. "We're about to become useful. Let's clean up this control center and get our crew uniforms on with the cravats, too. Oh, everyone wear your sidearm, too. Try not to shoot yourselves in the foot."

Two hours later the topside gate phone rang, and the white light flashed on both consoles. For an RV change out, there was no way to use the underground tunnels. This had to be a convoy in the old style, which would be very noticeable to satellite photo imagery.

"Control center, this is the RV change-out team. Request permission to come to the entryway cage to authenticate."

"Roger, permission granted. Come in and authenticate."

Susan was watching the topside camera screen hanging above the communications console. She saw the RV convoy composed of a crane truck, RV on a flatbed, a lead and following truck with armed personnel wearing camouflage, and a Huey hovering at the rear of the convoy. The convoy was followed by an APC armed with a manned .50 cal. machine gun on top.

Susan went to the safe, took out the authenticator booklet, and opened it to the current date. She watched as a single person walked from the camouflaged gate to the entranceway. She released the outer door electronically, and the gentleman stepped inside a wire cage. On the other side of the next wire door, the steps continued down to the first blast door and the elevator, waiting three stories below the surface. Susan watched the man on another camera screen while he took out an authentication page and picked up a phone in the cage. If he authenticated wrong, he'd stay in the cage until an armed response team arrived.

The man spoke into the phone. "I authenticate ALPHA SIERRA TANGO, ZULU LIMA HOTEL."

"Correct," Susan replied. "Come on in."

The man opened the inner wire cage door after Susan unlocked it electronically. He let himself through the hydraulic blast doors and entered the control center. Robert and the crew were lined up on the inner side of the low-tech order bookcases, while the man came along on the other side of the gray metal bookcases.

He held out his hand to Robert.

"Michael Lemming, chief of RV Team 8. I assume you know why we're here. Standard RV change-out. The targeting team may be along in a couple hours. Or they may be able to load targets remotely. They'll load a new target coordinate into your guidance system."

"Pleased to meet you." Robert then went through a verbal maintenance safety checklist. "That's all I have. We'll monitor you on the net and we're equipped with the topside camera. I presume your

Huey will land on the access road and then escort you back with the removed RV?"

"That's right. Everything by the book. I'll head up, and we'll get to work. The targeting team will do the guidance check after they load the targets. I'll send two men down here to drop the Level 1 platforms and get to work unbolting the RV."

"Sounds good," Robert replied. He and the crew then watched as the topside team plugged three wires from a small square metal box with a keypad into an access panel flush with the ground beside the silo door. They then typed in a five-digit code and the silo door – weighing 760 tons and composed of steel and concrete – electronically rolled open.

In the meantime, the crane was positioned next to the silo opening and the RV flatbed parked beside it. The two men whom Roger had mentioned came down into the control center, and Robert went through the silo safety briefing again. That briefing was important, as there had been accidents. Afterward, the men went to Level 1 of the silo, lowered the work platforms, and started unbolting the RV from the missile stage 2. Shortly after, the crane picked up the RV and set it by the open silo door, then picked up the new RV and set it onto the missile. It then loaded the replaced RV into the flatbed truck, where it was tarped and secured. The team then prepared to depart.

****

MOS101708TUNA TO US101804DAD/AMANDA.

RUSSIANS COMING 7th GUARDS MOUNTAIN AIR ASSAULT DIVISION.

KRYMSK BASE. US CANADA BORDER VIA GANDER, SARNIA, TURN SOUTH AT SWEET GRASS, MT TO ATTACK. UNK WHEN.

The Deputy for Missile Intelligence took another chance to get word to Bryce Duncan and Amanda. This was a red-hot division with plenty of combat experience. The deputy didn't know when, but he suspected it would be within a week.

****

The president had made up his mind.

"Roger, let's not evacuate the government. Instead, go ahead and calculate an intersection point with the asteroid so all our missiles hit it simultaneously. Of course, the intersect angles will all be slightly different, but let's get them on target at the same time. And let's send our 400 Minuteman III missiles into the melee. I'll get on the phone to the heads of the other nuclear armed missile countries and sell them our plan to bust this thing up into pieces."

"Yes, sir. I'll get right on it and let you know when that intersection will occur. By the way, there's another weapon you can try that's under development that involves a few of the hidden Titan 2 missiles. It's a theoretical laser on a Titan powerful enough to do great damage to surface targets such as air bases or cities. Perhaps it could be used against the asteroid."

"Pie in the sky? We've played with this before with little result except massive costs that my budget people had to hide from Congress. As far as new weapon systems go, the whole result has been a giant shit-show. Let's go with what we know is reliable. The old systems are often far more reliable than all this fancy new crap."

Ten minutes later, the president was on the phone again. "Julie, get me the director of the National Reconnaissance Center personally. Not an aide. And scramble the call."

At 3:15 p.m., the president's phone rang.

"Sir, the NRC Director is on the line."

"Thank you, Julie."

"Tim, how is your day?" asked the president.

"Always about to get worse when you call," the NRC director laughed.

"Tim, I have a Top-Secret job for your agency that needs to be kept under wraps. Absolutely no leaks. I want you to scan Colorado, Wyoming, and Utah from the air and see if you see any evidence of some sort of underground weapon system. Any pattern, movement, transport, people, supplies…anything out of the ordinary. Can you do that quickly?"

"Mr. President, we don't normally scan our own American land. The pictures will have to be as of today only."

"That's fine. I just need to know something today. Certainly within 24 hours. Will you use satellites?"

"No. There aren't any in stationary orbit there, and that would involve too many people. DARPA has a couple of old SR-71s they use for project testing still equipped with cameras. I think I can get one for a flyover, and Ft. Meade can develop and check the films using a tech or two. With the pilot, that's only three involved. I can have the report sent directly to me and I'll call you with the results."

"Thanks, Tim. I look forward to seeing them."

Later that night, a White House switchboard operator announced, "Mr. President, the Director of the NRC is calling."

"Thanks. Put him on, scrambled."

"Mr. President, this is the Director of the NRC."

"Tim, I see you're up late at the office, too," the president replied.

"Well, sir, you wanted fast results on that flyover out west. We had some computer help in seeing if there was anything interesting, plus a couple of bright young techs helped, too. I don't think we'd have found anything without the computer analysis of patterns."

"You did find something, then?"

"Not much. Just one odd thing. There are hunting cabins in the low hills of Wyoming, Colorado, and Utah. Not up in the mountains, just in the low rolling hills. Call them low foothills. They, meaning each cabin, appear different, each made of different materials. On their own, there's nothing to arouse any interest. But the computer did some math and pattern analysis, and there's something odd about the locations. When linked together with lines, those lines form a pattern."

"Tim, don't all lines form patterns?"

"Yes, of course. But these patterns of location repeat over distances of about 300 miles linking together 18 cabins in each pattern. In other words, a pattern of cabins in Colorado matches a pattern of cabin locations in Utah. It's spot-on. And the pattern is identical in Wyoming, too. There are three sets of 18; that's 54 cabins total. One would never see it since the distances are too great. But the computer program sees it from thousands of feet above, when the SR-71 took the film during its flyover. It can't be random, sir."

"Of course not. Please have your report over here in two hours. It's important. And Tim?"

"Yes?"

"This is absolutely hush-hush. No discussion of this ever, with anyone, including me. Never mention this again."

"Of course, Mr. President."

"Good night, then. Get some sleep."

Ten minutes later the phone rang again.

"Mr. President, I have the director of the National Security Agency calling," the operator said.

"Put him through."

"Good evening, Mr. President. I'm calling with the information you requested, and I also have input from the FBI and the CIA, as you asked."

"Great, Matthew. I appreciate the speedy call-back. Tell me what you found out about NASS."

"Well, sir, with only a few hours of investigation, and keeping limited numbers of people involved, the most important thing we found out is that NASS controls numerous smaller companies, all of them outside the US. Those companies are involved in lots of areas. Chemicals, transportation, computers, telescopes, metal fabrication, and others. They're often subcontractors in US government military projects. Many of the companies are being run by retired military officers, especially Air Force and Army. We don't have the details of what resources they buy or whom they sell to, but they appear to buy overseas and sell to the US government. Some of those sales involve classified black projects we can't access. They appear to be run by the Pentagon."

"I see. Matt, this is completely off the record, and we never discussed this. But do you think NASS has the capability to be maintaining any sort of liquid-fueled missile system?"

"Hmm. Maybe. There are some fuel and oxidizer purchases in Spain listed under research testing. NASS could be placing fresh fuel and oxidizer on a limited number of missiles every year, but why would they do so without a DoD contract?"

"They may have one I don't know about. Anyway, thanks for the info and keep this to yourself. Call me back if you uncover anything else. I'll need any new information within a couple days."

"Roger that, Mr. President. Will do."

****

The next day, the president spoke with Mr. Kyle O'Connell in the USAF HQ budget office.

"Hello, Mr. President. Kyle O'Connell here in the Pentagon Air Force budget office. I'm the senior comptroller for all weapons and maintenance projects. How may I help you?"

"Mr. O'Connell, I don't have time to explain, but I want a listing of all Air Force black project contracts with civilian companies being run by retired officers. I'm sure you have that information."

"Yes, I do, but are you sure you want to review it? There's the issue of plausible deniability to consider. If the press asks questions, sometimes it's best not to know about a funded project. Plus, across the USAF budget, we're talking about hundreds of projects ranging from a local lab project costing thousands of dollars at a small college to a major Defense Applied Research Project Agency project costing billions."

The president sighed. *If I hear "plausible deniability" one more time...* "Look, Mr. O'Connell, can you or can you not get me a list of every company and the retired officers in those companies involved in USAF black ops funded projects?"

"Yes, sir. We can. Of course, subsidiary companies may exist that would make things hard to track."

"Look for a company called NASS. And could you track through all USAF black projects if you looked at expense items for Aerozine 50, which is a 50/50 mix of hydrazine and UDMH, and nitrogen tetroxide, an oxidizer? I do remember my college chemistry classes. And Mr. O'Connell, I want you to go back 20 years. Use that big-ass computer sitting in the Pentagon. I'll have Julie fax over a personal authorization from me for priority access. I want to know if some company has been buying those chemicals for years under a black government contract. If there are too many to review, then concentrate on NASS and subsidiaries. Can you also see how many of those companies are buying missile fuel and oxidizer over the last 20 years?"

"Yes, Mr. President. We can pull that information, especially with the Pentagon computers. I'll get right on it."

Two hours later, while the president was looking at some websites about cataclysmic asteroid strikes on Earth, Julie walked in with a handful of budget data.

"Here you are, Mr. President. Mr. O'Connell faxed these over for you to see."

"Did you look at these?"

Julie looked mildly offended. "No, sir. Never do. Would probably make me worry more," she said.

The president took the stack of printouts and the synopsis report and started reading. He highlighted passages with a yellow marker. Every time he underlined something, he thought of the captain in *The Caine Mutiny* throwing over the yellow dye marker by the beach. Using stick glue, he cut up and pasted relevant sections as related by threads on the Oval Office wall, creating a summary of Mr. O'Connell's findings:

-NASS is staffed with numerous retired military officers, especially with grades 0-6 and higher. Its entire Board of Directors is retired military grade 0-7 and higher.

-Since 1970, NASS has consistently bought missile fuel and oxidizer compatible with Titan II.

-There have been hijackings of tanker trucks carrying fuel and oxidizer in America. NASS may have been taking those missile propellants for real missiles.

-Through subcontractor trucking firms, fuel and oxidizer has been trucked from Gulf Coast factories in Lake Charles, Louisiana and Vicksburg, Mississippi to Utah, Wyoming, and Colorado. After crossing state borders, final delivery locations couldn't be determined. However, destination addresses filed during loading apparently were all fabricated. This office could not find one destination on shipping documents that had received any such shipment, and the addresses, if businesses, had no requirements for fuel or oxidizer. The cost to load Stage 1 and 2 of one Titan II is approximately $1,380,000. The fuel and oxidizer could sit in the missile for an indefinite time. Usually fuel and oxidizer removal was due to some other component needing replacement. Both chemicals' costs were reimbursed by the government to NASS from various budgets, all classified. As such, none of the costs were questioned.

-NASS, through subsidiaries, bought considerable crew supplies in bulk such as food, drink, dried rations, bedding, uniforms, tools, test equipment, entertainment, weapons, ammunition, replacement parts, etc. Annual costs were hundreds of thousands of dollars, all coming from classified budgets.

-There is evidence that this Titan project, through the assistance of senior government fiscal resource managers, was consistently funded starting in the 1960s by "raiding" the Social Security Administration Emergency Fund, which has never been used except by NASS. That action was illegal as Congress did not approve of such a funds transfer. This action has been directly contributing to Social Security programs running out of money.

-NASS is sponsoring a classified human rejuvenation project apparently for volunteers involved in the Titan project. This project is attempting goals and methods deemed unethical by the United Nations Council on Human Development. It could earn the US a considerable condemnation from other nations.

-There exists sufficient financial and document evidence to turn over materials to the Justice Department for criminal prosecution of numerous high-level retired officers and government civilian employees for managing such a project without the approval of Congress unless such a project and budgeting are classified. A multitude of laws have been broken on both a company and individual level, and apparently continue to be broken.

"Well, what a scandal we have here," the president muttered to himself. "Time to talk to the big dogs."

He picked up the phone.

"Julie, please locate Generals Clegg and Birmingham. If we're lucky, both are in Washington right now. I'd like to speak to both at the same time."

Thirty minutes later, the desk phone buzzed.

"Sir, General Clegg and General Birmingham are both on the line. Both are here in Washington."

"Thank you, Julie."

"Gentlemen, how are you today?" he began.

"Fine, sir," both replied.

"There's a matter of some urgency I wish to discuss with both of you. Since you're here in Washington, could you come to the White House in an hour? Use the Secret Service entrance in the rear, not the normal visitor entrance. Unless there's an overriding reason not to be here, I'll expect you both in an hour."

Less than an hour later, there was a knock on the door.

"Come in," the president said.

He shook hands with Generals Clegg and Birmingham.

"Please be seated. There isn't time for pleasantries, so I'll get to the point. I've been checking up on you two. As best as I could, I've confirmed that you two have been the key players in the arming and launch preparations of 54 Titan II missiles with nuclear warheads in Colorado, Wyoming, and Utah. We'll hold off on discussing the legal violations involved in this over the years, at least for the time being. Honestly speaking, these missiles could end up saving humanity's ass from that asteroid heading toward us. What I want from the both of you right now is a tour of one of the silos. Not pictures and slides, but an actual tour of a silo. I'll have one of our fastest planes standing by at Andrews AFB. It's up to you which silo we visit, but I want to go now, then right back here."

General Birmingham answered, "Sir, we could go to a silo one hour west of Denver off I-70. Total travel time there and back would be about six hours round trip. You could get some sleep on the way. I presume we're going in Air Force One?" The two generals nodded, knowing how comfortable Air Force One was.

"No, I've done better than Air Force One. You two aren't the only ones to play the shell game. Have you two ever flown at 2,200 miles an hour? No? We can be in Wyoming, which has less air traffic than Colorado, in an hour. It'll take a week for your stomach to catch up. I did it once when I was in the Guard. I was considering whether to try for a pilot slot in one of the squadrons. After that experience, I didn't apply. But it's a great way to travel very fast when needed. Do you know how we're going?"

"The SR-71?" asked General Birmingham.

"You got it. There are three of them landing now at Andrews. You know where I had these three hidden away in storage with only a maintenance team and four pilots around? Those pilots retired when the USAF retired the planes in 1998. They then went to work in a special presidential transportation unit. Every president since the planes' retirement has had those three available if he needed them. So which airport are we going to for this jaunt?"

"The best option then is Laramie, Wyoming," General Birmingham replied. "Land on runway 21 at 8,502 feet in length. That airport has a Wyoming ANG unit there flying C-130H models. It's a very nice airport. We can park on Taxiway C, over by the fire station. Maybe in the dark we won't be noticed. The unit there is the 153 Airlift Wing, Wyoming Air National Guard. If we need it, they can provide all sorts of support. Their HQ is actually down at Cheyenne at the Cheyenne ANG base, but they do plenty of activity at Laramie."

"Okay," said the president. "That means we're heading to a Wyoming silo. You choose. Oh, I forgot to tell you where I hid those three planes. I bet you thought it was in the Arizona boneyard. No! They sit in an old, rusted WWII hangar with Army Air Corp 'Do Not Trespass' signs all around it. My people only transit in or out at night, same for any maintenance people or equipment and parts. It's at a place I like to fish called Devils Lake, North Dakota. We have some Minuteman missiles on alert there, ready to go. Nice airport. I sometimes go look at my planes without any secret service along to scare the fish. Who would think those incredible planes are stored two miles from an amazing lake filled with some of the biggest pike and bass you'll ever see? I'll have my staff set up a rental car and one of you can drive."

The President picked up the phone before the three left. "Operator, get me the senior secret service officer on White House duty tonight."

There was a pause, then "Good evening, Mr. President. I'm Duke Carter, the senior White House secret service officer on duty tonight."

"Good, Mr. Carter. I wanted you to know that I and Generals Clegg and Birmingham are going on a secret trip. General Birmingham is carrying the nuclear codes case. We'll be back by dawn. If anything earth-shattering happens tonight, call my private number. Otherwise, let the vice president handle it or let it wait until morning. I can't tell you where we're going, but it's not in the local area. Please pass this on to my family for me since we have to leave right now. I'm having an Army chopper pick us up and we're going over to Andrews AFB. After that, knowledge is restricted. There will be no secret service on this trip. Good night."

"Good night, Mr. President," Duke replied. "Safe travels."

They rode flew to Andrews AFB in a National Guard Black Hawk helicopter. Upon landing, they could see the three SR-71s in a row. "Gentlemen, take your pick," the president said. "I'll ride in the third one."

With some help, the three slipped into the planes. They took off in a cluster on runway 1R at 9,756 feet. The climb out was terrific, and they flew clustered together on autopilot.

As the three SR-71s took off, the technical sergeant in the control tower, which had been cleared of all personnel except him and an airman first class, commented, "These goes a sight you may never see again in your life, and better sure never talk about. Get me?"

"Yes, Sergeant. I've forgotten about it already. Definitely something I never expected to see. The Only SR-71 I ever saw was at the Dayton Airforce Museum, just sitting there. These planes seem so full of life. And *three* of them. I wonder who was on board in the rear seats."

****

Wyoming. Silo 3-7.

The red phone rang in the control center, and Robert answered it. The ringing of the red phone was such a rare event that the other three crew members watched while Robert listened. After he hung up, he turned to them. "We have visitors coming from Washington. Apparently high-powered types. Let's get our visitor uniforms on and straighten up.

They're apparently traveling in something very fast, as they'll be here in less than two hours. Let's shake a leg."

The three SR-71s landed at Laramie and pulled down to Taxiway C behind a white airport security pickup truck with a "Follow Me" sign mounted over the cab. Their rental car was waiting by the fire station with the key fob on the driver's seat. General Birmingham drove since he knew where silo 3-7 was located, and the way in through the cabin. Upon arriving at the silo station, the general said, "If you'll step this way, Mr. President, you'll see what's going to stop this asteroid."

The men walked into the cabin, furnished with a table, chairs, living room furniture, and the usual kitchen clutter. General Birmingham led the way to a closet door with a pattern of wooden panels. He pressed four of the square panels on the door, then opened it to reveal an elevator inside. This elevator was a secret new addition, not used by contractors, and not from the original design. "It's a tight fit, gentlemen, but this will take us down to the missile control center," he said.

After a 20-second ride, the doors opened into a concrete room containing two massive blast doors on hinges, with twelve-inch pins holding them closed. Stepping to the right door, General Birmingham picked up the phone to the left of the door and said: "Visitors Alpha, Delta, Zulu."

In the launch control room, Robert pressed the button marked "Door 8 Open," and the pins securing the seven-ton door withdrew. Both generals pulled the door open, and the president led the way into the control room where Robert, Susan, Jeff, and Sandy waited in a line to greet their special guests.

General Birmingham introduced the crew to the president and General Clegg, reading their names from their crew name patches. For the president, he explained the roles of the crew commander, deputy commander, BMAT, and MFT. He also explained the three levels of the manned area of the silo. Level 1 was the living area; Level 2 (where they were now) contained launch and monitoring equipment, a weather station, communication gear, a TV and lounge area, emergency breathing masks (in case of a fuel or oxidizer leak), revolvers, and the commander's complex control panel; Level 3 had communications gear, emergency rations, and the hatch to the crew emergency escape ladder to the surface.

The president said, "Well, can I actually go see this missile?"

"Of course, sir," General Clegg replied.

Robert spoke up. "Before we go out to the silo, you should know how to don these emergency oxygen masks in case we encounter a fuel or oxidizer leak. The chances are very low, but you should know. Sensors would detect a leak long before it would affect us. Perhaps one of the crew would demonstrate."

Sandy took out the demonstrator mask and showed how to don and activate the mask in case of emergency. Then the three, accompanied by Jeff, walked over to the blast door and waited while the locking pins retracted. After passing through and closing the door behind them, they again waited while the pins retracted on Door 9. Opening this door and securing it behind them, they faced a long hallway leading to the missile. The hallway was lit with fluorescent lights. At the end of the hallway, which continued around the central concrete core of the missile area, was a five-foot door latched shut. Jeff opened the latch and pressed a series of buttons which hydraulically lowered open grating platforms around the missile, allowing one to walk to the other side of it for maintenance.

"Sir," Jeff said, "it looks scary being eight stories up from the bottom of the missile, but it's perfectly safe to walk out here and look up at the warhead. You may be happier if you don't look down."

The president walked out onto the grating and looked up at the missile's nose cone, then glanced downward.

"This thing is immense," he marveled. "I can't believe there are 53 more like this one, ready to launch."

"Yes, sir. Fifty-four total, all the same as we once had on active alert status," General Clegg replied. "Launch time is about three minutes by the time the crew opens the red safe, decodes the launch message, inserts the keys and turns, and the missile gets going. After the key turn, the actual launch sequence takes about a minute."

The president nodded. "And I was never to know about these 54 missiles?"

"No, sir. These are America's ace in the hole. Plausible deniability on your part, but you would've been told – as you *were* told – in a true emergency like this one, or a world war. And don't forget, the Navy has operational long-range missile boats sitting on the bottom of the oceans in storage that aren't on any active duty rosters. This gives America hundreds more warheads for such emergencies."

"I find it incredible," the president replied, "that such an operation could continue for years with no press leaks or anyone blabbing. As I said, these extra warheads have destroyed our honor with foreign countries by violating international treaties – but they just might save our bacon."

"Yes, sir," replied General Birmingham. "We're counting on it."

"Perhaps you'd like to see a very impressive sight, sir," General Clegg suggested. "Even more impressive than looking at the warhead. If you'll follow me, sir, you'll see something you'll never forget."

The group exited the launch duct and entered a small elevator. Jeff pressed "9" and the elevator rode quietly to the bottom of the silo.

General Clegg said, "Sir, if you'll accompany me onto a small platform and look up, it's a sight you'll remember for the rest of your life."

Jeff again opened a door latch, and the general led the way through. The president stepped through next and looked up. Over their heads were the two enormous Titan coned engines.

"My God, they're *huge*," the president exclaimed. "Tell me some specs. This is truly amazing."

The general noted the technical details. "Stage 1 engines, which you're looking at, produce 430,000 pounds of thrust, while Stage 2 does 100,000 pounds of thrust. The missile is 103 feet tall with a 10-foot diameter. It weighs 170,000 tons. The original warhead was a W-53 inside a Mark 6 reentry vehicle with a force of 9 megatons. It was a *hell* of a reliable weapon system for a nuclear war."

The President took it all in, then looked down. "What's that below us? All that concrete in the shadows?"

"It's called what it looks like, sir: the "W." It's where the engine exhaust goes. Down, then up through ducts up the sides of the silo to the surface. It's to prevent the missile from being destroyed by its own exhaust before it gets out of the silo, since the exit speed from the silo is rather slow. That "W" is what gives Titan II its notable twin plume of exhaust at the surface. Any video or photos taken of Titan II show that twin plume, while Minutemen missiles have just a single exhaust ring cloud and much faster acceleration out of the silo."

"And yet we had some accidents. I seem to remember two of them."

"Yes, sir. The oxidizer leak at Wichita and the silo explosion at Little Rock. And 53 died during a construction accident. These liquid fueled missiles weren't foolproof. It took dedicated ops and maintenance crews to operate and maintain them. Dedication is the watchword out here."

The president returned to the control center along with the two generals and Jeff, and took a seat on one of the television recliners. He motioned to the crew to gather around. Robert marveled at the whole situation: the president of the country and two of his generals, all gathered in a missile silo with its crew. Just four ordinary people visiting with the most powerful people in the US. It felt surreal, to say the least.

"Thanks for your hospitality," the president remarked. "It's not often we three get to spend much time with regular folks outside DC. If you don't mind talking informally, I think we could learn some things from you. Tell me, do you really think that missile down the hall can fly, or do you think it'll just fly apart? I'd like to hear from each of you."

Robert began. "Sir, I think it'll go. Maintenance has replaced parts as proscribed, the electronic circuits all passed the self-checks, and there's nothing physically awry. It's ready to fly. Corrosion control has been done, and there's nothing wrong with its structure. I think it'll go."

Susan was next, going in order of seniority. "I agree with Robert. I can't think of any reason why it wouldn't fly. I have little time in Titan at this point, but I believe if there's no discernible reason why it won't go, then it *will*."

Sandy commented, "From my expertise, the guidance system is reasonably good. Sure, it's not as accurate as today's systems, but it'll hit within a half-mile."

"I think they've done a good job of corrosion control," Jeff noted, "but I worry that somewhere there's a brittle bolt, a loose nut – something small that'll doom the missile as it takes off. If our enemies knew when we were launching, they might shoot it with a rifle enough to make the fuel and oxidizer tanks leak, which would cause a huge explosion. Its departure from the silo is slow, and there were a few Titan failures in the Gemini program. I don't think it'll make it to Stage 1 separation."

The president nodded, said thanks and farewell to the crew, and headed back to the White House.

Chapter 12: Complications

The Oval Office the following day.

"Mr. President, here are more pardons for you to sign as part of your prisoner amnesty and rehabilitation program. Another 10 ready to go."

"Thank you, Julie. You're putting in a long day." He looked at her. It would be a shame to lose a good secretary to an asteroid.

"Julie, I'd like you to do something, but you have to keep it to yourself, okay?"

"Of course."

"We may have to take a short-notice trip somewhere. Pack two travel bags for yourself, one for here and one for home so you're prepared to leave on very short notice either way."

"May I ask where I might be going?"

"I'm not quite sure. Maybe the Maryland mountains or the Cheyenne Mountain complex."

She nodded. "Survival places. Is there a threat?"

He looked at her, wanting to share the news while knowing he couldn't.

"You know better than to ask. Just be ready. We wouldn't want to lose you, okay?"

"That serious? Was this related to your visitors this morning?"

He couldn't help but chuckle. "Well, bless their souls, everything in this country is related to them. I'm sorry, Julie, I can't tell you any more just yet."

A short time later, the president greeted Le Yobo, the Chinese Ambassador, and Sergi Kasinki, the Russian Ambassador. Both spoke excellent English, Le having graduated from Princeton and Sergi from Cambridge. "Welcome, gentlemen. Please help yourself to drinks and let's sit together. The English and French Ambassadors will be here in a minute."

There was a knock at the door, and Alice Tinhouse, the English Ambassador, and Villard Homecourt, the French Ambassador, entered and accepted drinks.

"Folks, sometimes in the world there comes a crisis so important that diplomacy is irrelevant. I'm reminded of a favorite book of mine called *Kabloona* by Gontran de Poncins. It's about a Frenchman who goes to the arctic to live with Eskimos and discovers that the essence of life is to be a human, preeminently. That wealth, power, and things mean little to the quality of life. In truth, he discovers that community, being human, being part of a family – *that's* what matters. So, let's consider that we, here, are a community of five. We come from different cultures, with different goals. But at the base of a triangle, what keeps the triangle from falling is common ground and shared goals. And the basic human goal is *survival*. Nothing else. Do we agree so far?"

The room was silent. *Well, at least no one* disagrees *so far,* the president thought.

"I ask each of you, before I speak of what I wish to confer with you about, have your scientists noticed anything unusual in the skies? Something catastrophic. Speak up so we can work together against a common threat."

The men looked at each other and nodded.

Lo spoke first. "Our scientists informed me today of final disaster for the earth. I assume that is the crisis you're referring to."

Sergi nodded. "Yes, I was told early this morning. There is little doubt it will either hit the planet or come close enough to boil much of the oceans and waters of the earth away, resulting in complete climate disaster. We've begun quietly evacuating the government from Moscow and disbursing our nuclear warheads and some delivery systems, as I'm sure you and our Chinese friends are also, as are the French and English, I presume. We think it best not to tell everyone, as that would cause panic and hoarding. It's best to see where it hits and who survives, then try to reconstruct society from there."

The five men sipped their drinks and thought a moment. The president spoke next.

"Gentlemen, what I'm going to tell you must absolutely remain with us five. The political repercussions are grave, the consequences unpredictable. That's why I asked that we meet with just the five of us together. No translators or secretaries or aides. Just the five of us. Now, I've have been told this morning that without my authorization and knowledge, and without the knowledge of any American president, the United States has at its disposal 540 additional M-53 warheads on missiles ready to launch."

Sergi jumped to his feet.

"Mr. President, you mean the U.S. has hidden 540 active alert warheads? Targeted, no doubt, at China and Russia. That's a violation of all the SALT treaties and our public agreements. It's disgraceful! This negates all the arms reductions agreements. It means the US lied about the number of active warheads. Why should any country stay in an arms reduction treaty with the US after this?"

The president sat calmly.

"That's correct. I was never told of this, and if you want me to, I can produce the retired general in charge of the program who managed it. I was as shocked as you are, and those responsible can be brought to justice. They've admitted their guilt. It means the US misrepresented everything about arms reductions. I've also discovered that many more weapon systems were never deactivated. Systems for the Army and Navy. For example, the Pershing nuclear tactical system exists, despite programs to deactivate it. I admit to deception, and I myself was duped by a few key people. Nevertheless, in a few days none of this will matter unless we fire every long-range missile we have at this asteroid to deflect it from its path toward us."

Sergi shook his head.

"Our scientists say the nations of the earth don't possess enough nuclear power to accomplish this. We need hundreds of additional warheads, even counting what the French and English can launch from their submarines, as well as from American submarines. You're saying these newly discovered, highly convenient warheads of yours may give us the firepower we need?"

Villard commented, "Mr. President, I think we can all agree to let the recriminations and accusations wait until after this crisis has passed. But if we survive it, the US government should face the consequences of its actions. I would believe this marks the end of your administration, and the careers of several military leaders."

The ambassadors nodded. Not one urged the president to stay in office. Ignorance certainly wasn't bliss.

Like sharks in bloody water, the president mused to himself. *I'm surprised they all agreed to wait 'til this is over.*

****

Wyoming. Silo 3-7.

One night, while Sandy and Robert were on the control center (Level 2), Susan and Jeffrey were doing equipment checks out in the silo. Sandy and Robert were sitting side-by-side in two armchairs, watching the Army football team getting walloped by the University of

Cincinnati's team. Sandy said, "Robert, we've met before. Do I look familiar?"

"Well, actually, no. I don't recall that we've ever met. And the colonel would never put a couple on a crew if one were assigned as someone else's mate."

"Gillette, New Jersey. A Halloween party long ago, in a grange hall community center. I wore my hair black then, with blond streaks. I wore a witch's costume. We went out on the porch and kissed, and a week later we had sex together in your grandfather's barn near Morristown. And I was using the long form of my name. When my mom remarried, I switched my last name to match hers. When I was at that party, I was Sandra Morrison. After I took her new last name and shortened my first name, I became Sandy Stewart. Do you remember Sandra Morrison?"

Robert and Sandy's first kiss was beneath this Grange Hall sign in Gillette, New Jersey. It's still there at 500 Meyersville Road.

"Remember? I still picture you in the loft. You were my first girl. Sometimes I wondered where you were after your mom and you moved away from Gillette. But you know how things are. People get busy with living and don't pursue these things."

He stared at her.

"Yes, I can still see you in there behind an older face."

He held out his hand to her and she took it.

"I'm surprised the colonel's team missed this," he said. "I guess the name change and moving when you were young just stayed under the radar."

"And here we are, years later, sitting for five years in a missile silo." She looked at him. "Wanna renew an old friendship? Being with Jeffery is already boring. Now I remember why I broke up with him in college. He's just so *boring*. I think the colonel's team missed that, too."

"You mean you want a romantic friendship like we had in high school?"

"Yes, like before you met Susan. I was surprised as hell when I found out I was paired with Jeffery. Of all the guys I knew, he was the least romantic."

"God, Sandy, this idea you have could wreck the whole plan."

"Well, you can't program human variables and nature. We make choices that can't be planned for. Look at it this way. We four are on this silo complex for five years with the same people. There are two guys here courtesy of our government: you and Jeffrey. He's boring. That leaves you, and it's not like we just met. We slept together years ago. So, I'm asking. I'll put this frankly. Jeff doesn't interest or satisfy me. You do, and I know from high school you're a great lay. Wouldn't you like to have both of us girls?"

"And what happens when Jeff finds out his commander is sleeping with his assigned mate? What happens when Susan finds out? This could wreck the whole experiment."

"He'll probably quit, and I'll be assigned someone else I knew a long time ago. Don't feel abandoned if that happens; I'll still sleep with both of you. Otherwise, I'm gonna have a dull five years down here. Being bored that long may not be worth a million dollars to me."

"Why didn't you speak up before we were sent down here?"

"I didn't think it would be as dull as it is with him. I guess I'd forgotten how happy I was to break up with him. It was a long time ago. We tend to forget troubling things. Maybe the government is using us and the other crews to see how four-person units would live together on Mars. Maybe this isn't about Titan at all, but how people interact during long space flights and when living in limited social environments on Mars or the moon. What a great way to study us. We think we're doing this to help America – which we are – but we're thinking of Earth while the scientists are thinking of us on Mars."

Robert sighed, feeling suddenly overwhelmed. "Maybe. Let me think about your offer. There could be a lot of unforeseen effects and consequences with us having a relationship. The other two would likely be jealous. Things could get ugly and even violent. We can't have that."

The hum of the air blowers, the aircraft radio net chatter, the teletype clattering, an occasional voice transmission by the command center all made it seem like a normal alert. Yet, the ominous totality of five years hung over them all. Was it worth giving five years of one's life for a million dollars? None of the others seemed to know, but Robert could tell Sandy was already leaning toward quitting soon and leaving the silo. That meant they'd get a replacement. What if others quit? What if their only options of being in the silo or spending limited time topside made them all unstable at some point? What if one of them went nuts? There were four loaded .38-caliber pistols in the gray metal cabinet just a few feet from the chairs they were sitting in. What would it do to trust between them if he started wearing his sidearm? What if Susan wore hers, too? *Not a very good way to boost morale,* Robert thought. There'd likely be serious trouble if they weren't monogamous to their assigned mates. Group sex would undermine any sense of mission or discipline, and Jeff certainly didn't seem like the "swinger" type. Truth be told, Robert wasn't exactly sure of his own feelings on the matter. He was all but certain, however, that switching partners deceitfully would ruin everything, and they could end up killing each other. This had already happened with other crews, and the possibility couldn't be ignored. *Christ,* he thought. *What a way to meet your maker. Why does everything have to be so complicated? I have to think of a way for Sandra to be happy with Jeff. That's not gonna be easy...*

He knew part of the problem was that no matter how much the place was beautified, it was still an old missile silo. They could go topside now, but not off the complex. He suspected there were cameras to make sure they all stayed put and didn't go wandering off. Still, there had to be a way to raise the morale of his team before they grew to hate each other.

****

They celebrated Jeff's birthday in the silo with a nice dinner of clams, steak, and wine, but there was little to say. By now, they'd heard each other's stories to the point they could finish each other's sentences. They were growing bored with each other. They'd gradually taken to using each other's favorite sayings and phrases, yet while their language was composed increasingly of each other's words, they weren't coalescing into a unified crew. There was a long way to go for their million-dollar bonus, and Robert, based on his crew commander experience, didn't think they'd ever mold well into a team. The rejuvenation process, he reasoned, had left them all at 19 years old, and without variation in age and maturity, they were apathetic, bored, and self-absorbed – the common drags of being a teenager. *Life* sucks, *man,* he thought with a wry smile.

He made it a point to stay away from Sandy, but he was very much concerned that her lack of satisfaction with Jeff would spell big-time trouble. One day, he thought of a way for everyone to alleviate their boredom for awhile. *Contacting and chatting with the other silos on HF through the 80-foot-high antenna could be a big morale builder,* he figured. *What do we have to lose?*

"Susan, this is your area. Look in the safe and find the HF frequency list for the other silos. Let's chat with our neighbors a bit."

Susan sat in front of the two-drawer gray safe and flicked through the folder tabs. About halfway through, she pulled out a laminated list of silo numbers, call signs, and HF frequencies in the 6-30 MHz range. She then dialed in the frequency of the next silo in numbered sequence.

"Bison 12, Bison 12, this is Bison 11. How do you read?" she called.

There was silence.

"Bison 12, Bison 12, this is Bison 11. How do you read?" she repeated.

"Bison 11, this is 12," a women replied.

"Twelve, where are you guys? Are there four of you?"

"Elven, I'm sorry. I don't think we should chat about that. This isn't a secure frequency."

"Twelve, how's the view from where you are?"

"Eleven, flat and boring. No one within 50 miles. Like being stationed in hell. You?"

"Twelve, closeup of mountains, lots of trees. What else can we talk about?"

"Eleven, not much to say, but good to know you're out here, too."

"Try calling the Alternate Command Post," Robert said. "Let's talk to them."

Susan looked in the laminated sheet and dialed in the new frequency. "Rook 2, Rook 2, this is Bison 11. How do you read?" she called. After a moment of silence, she repeated herself.

"Bison 11, this is Rook 2. What do you need?"

"Rook 2, we'd like to not be bored. Can you help with that?" She laughed into the mic.

"Sorry, 11. It's part of missile life. Long periods of boredom punctuated by minutes of terror that everything's going straight to hell. You'll get used to it."

Susan didn't know how to reply.

"Eleven, anything more?"

"Rook 2, no. Thank you. Eleven out."

She turned to Robert. "Well, our companions aren't very talkative. But at least they're out here with us."

"Maybe," Robert said. "Maybe. We'll never really know."

"Come on, let's play canasta," Sandy said excitedly. "Someone go get four cans of beer. We're civilians, remember? Let's live a litle."

"Oh, piss off."

"*You* piss off. Deal the cards!"

"What the fuck is this hand?"

"Fry me some Rocky Mountain oysters."

"Eww, gross. Pass me a beer."

"This is purgatory, not hell. Hell is when the oxidizer leaks. Remember that, people."

"Yeah, yeah. Whose deal is it?"

"Try not to deal me the worst hand in Wyoming. You suck at dealing."

"You suck at *life*!"

"There was a young lady in Niger. She rode on the back of the tiger. Who walked with a smile, who dressed in great style. So then she ended up inside her."

"Who?"

"The tiger, you fool. She ended up in the tiger."

"What the hell? Where the hell'd you hear that?"

"Deal, will you?"

"Okay, keep your pants on. Someone turn on some music."

And so the night passed among these guardians of free will and random choices.

****

Night shift.

Robert was stretched out with his ankles up on the end of the launch console and Jeff was watching *A Werewolf in Paris* when there was a loud snap of a main breaker opening on the equipment control panel. Everything but battery-powered indicator lights suddenly went dark.

"Well, fuck me over in the clover," Jeff said. "Must be a storm up there. That's weird. The periscope eyes didn't show any lightning."

Robert was quietly counting seconds. When he got to 30 one-thousand, a green light lit on the facilities panel. The lights did not come on, but neither did the diesel generator. That was a good sign.

"Commercial power available," Robert said.

"Commercial power available," Jeff confirmed before snapping a large breaker in the panel up. The lights and other gear powered back on.

Robert looked at his watch. Two hours to shift change and a real bed. And maybe some real scrambled eggs. He made a log entry about the power loss, then stretched out, watching the second hand on the clock above the communication console. *How many seconds has it clicked since this place was built,* he wondered. *When will it click its last?*

****

Amanda had devoted a lot of thought (computer processing) to the Russian attack scenario, after which she called General Birmingham at his home in Virginia on a scrambled government line. She chose Synthetic Voice #8 as the most reassuring to the general.

"Hello General, this is Amanda. I'm sorry to bother you but we have a crisis. Russian Missile Intelligence has found our LGM25-Cs. I believe a Russian airborne expedition will try to destroy all of them by blowing up the underground fuel and oxidizer piping system. Those pipes are interconnected without check- or shut-off valves except at the very end. If they blow the fuel and oxidizer pipes at one silo, all 54 will subsequently explode."

The general frowned. "Can we stop this?"

"We can't stop the attack once it's underway at the destination silo, which will likely be one of the northernmost silos of the 54. And we can't fight a limited ground war without the press and public eventually finding out about the 54 hidden missiles. I believe we may have to take our licks this time. Do you have any ideas?"

General Birmingham thought for a moment. "Actually, yes. In the 1950s and 1960s, the US fielded an anti-aircraft system called the Nike Hercules ground-to-air missile. There were lots of variants and over 100 launch sites mostly protecting cities from Russian bombers. In league with the other hidden and preserved weapon systems that are still operational, we have a Nike Hercules missile operational from 1959 still at Roberts, Wisconsin near the Twin Cities. It's site MS-20 with a crew of elderly veterans sustaining one missile. That missile has a 90-mile range up to 100,000 feet at Mach 4. Those missiles were on alert in Europe until 1988.

"The downside is that there's a dead zone of 10,000 yards distance and 20,000 feet of altitude. A low-flying plane can't be hit. But bombers, due to fuel inefficiency, rarely fly attack missions low. If the Russians fly through that Nike window of opportunity, we can kill everyone on the plane. We can shoot down their plane, and no one will ever know how we did it. They'll only be able to tell it was an external explosion. Call that site and explain the situation to them as I laid it out. They'll get no official recognition for their valor, unfortunately, but we *need* them. And Amanda…"

"Yes, General?"

"Pretty soon it won't matter. All 54 are probably going to be launched against this asteroid."

"Noted. I'll set everything up, including the radar tracking from three radar sites for the Nike," Amanda replied.

"One other thing," said the general. "You don't know, but in the Arizona airplane boneyard there's a hidden operational squadron of Vietnam-era ANG F-4 Phantom fighters with pilots, fuel, armament, and maintenance all set up. I'll give you their contact number. Set two F-4s up at a small civilian airport close to the border with a hard-surfaced runway. If anyone notices them, our cover story is we're doing a commemorative reenactment flight. If the Russians are out of missile range, the two Phantoms can get them. They're all-weather, 1,700-mile range, supersonic, with air-to-air missiles. Check the needed runway length. I think it's 4,900 feet. Set it up if you need them. Oh, and be sure fuel is attainable."

"Yes, General. I'll take care of it. And I'll watch Russian communication for the mission date."

Amanda's alertness paid off. Soon after her call to General Birmingham, she intercepted voice communications from the attacking Russian unit and was able to calculate their departure date. She then sent an encrypted message to the general, alerting him of this.

Chapter 13: Sex and Paratroopers

Susan and Robert were topside looking at stars, sitting next to each other in beach chairs. She had her hand over his, both resting on the aluminum arm of the chair. "Are you bored out here?" she asked.

Robert thought a moment and sighed. "Yeah. There's only so much television to watch, or stories to tell the same three people, or board games to play. When the colonel proposed this job, those 60 months sitting in an old missile seemed like a great way to capture and relive our past. To share a life together we otherwise wouldn't have. It seemed like heaven to me. Now I see the four of us turning inward with our thoughts like we're in solitary confinement. Those five years are starting to seem more like time behind bars than a happy, fun time together."

"Are you bored with me, too?" she asked.

"No, you're still the light in my life, and I hope any unhappiness I might feel won't affect things between us. I hoped you'd come back for years. And here we are. I don't take that for granted. How about you?"

"I feel washed away. There isn't much to do. As old as the missile is, I thought there'd be more equipment failures. And even when there is a problem, maintenance sends out parts and a repair team, so we learn nothing new about the equipment. I have no sense of purpose at all. Sitting here day after day waiting for a launch command that may never come. It's just so boring and frustrating," she said.

"Maybe that's why in the original Titan II, the alerts were just 24 hours. I think there was some plan in Minuteman that stretched the length of alerts in return for fewer of them in total. I know the plan wasn't adopted after the trials were evaluated. I wonder if that was due to a morale problem."

"Just think about when people go to Mars. The isolation they'll have to deal with."

"Perhaps what people need are better games and more excitement. More lethality," he laughed.

"Maybe more seemingly dangerous games so we're not bored."

She looked at him in the starlight. "You wanna make our bedtime games more lethal?"

He looked at her and grinned. "How?"

"Well, we could play out some prey-hunter scenarios. I'll be the prey. With a safe word for me."

"We could, but we'd have to play out here while the other two were in the control center, watching things. We'd have to disable the topside television camera. This could get rough out here since everything's pretty much steel and concrete. We could end up hurting ourselves."

She nodded slyly. "Makes things more dangerous to have metal and concrete everywhere. At least we wouldn't be bored."

"Maybe if we work together and listen to each other, we could do things without getting hurt. So, what's the scenario?"

"Damsel in distress trusts an evil gentleman who takes her honor and good name. Gets her pregnant. Let me control the pacing, okay? I can be the evil villainess."

"Go for it."

He stretched out on the ground ,letting her be the pathfinder. She continuously pressed her lips to his. They looked at each other as couples do when they're consumed with passion.

"Robert, I want to be your girl, forever. No regrets later. Travel with me on a mental trip. Give me all of your mind." She moved her hands over his upper arms. Her motions increased. Her tongue flicked between her parted lips. The diamond on her ring finger glistened in the occasional heat lightning. They kept their eyes on each other as she felt coiled and tense inside.

He reached up to tenderly brush his fingertips over each cheek. That touch to her cheek took her over a cliff on an accelerating drop. The rush was unlike anything she'd ever experienced. Like falling on an infinite roller coaster with disintegration roiling over her at the bottom of the ride. She felt wicked and female and oh so in control. She felt *alive.*

They both wailed, her higher-pitched cry echoing back from the forest. Their neural wiring, synapses, nerve endings, and tactile senses all melted together in a primal breathtaking overload. A massive flash of heat lightning arched above the concrete and steel silo door, and thunder rumbled around them.

Afterwards, they clung to each other, panting and shaking, her head on his chest, hands holding both of his tightly. Savoring the cool night air, she cuddled on top of him. She felt dizzy and disoriented, and she clung to him.

"God, there's no one like you. I'm so glad we're here together." She kissed his chest, feeling his heartbeat, content in his true and constant love for her. "I wonder if Food Services could deliver us ice cream?"

She was silent for a moment, then looked at him and commented, "You know a lot more about sex than you used to."

He laughed. "I read neurological fiction books now. But I hardly know what to do. I'm just a novice."

She scoffed. "Like *hell* you are."

****

The following day, out in the silo, Sandy walked up to Robert, looked at him, and in a husky voice asked, "Can I play dangerous games, too? Susan told me how you two are playing now to deal with boredom. Suppose we roleplay and talk through a storyline first? Suppose I really fight back some, hit you more than Susan does? Would you like that? What if I beg you to stop but we agree you won't. I wanna have the biggest bang ever. Could we please try? It's just so *boring* out here."

She quickly continued before he could respond. "We can use our minds to bring stories to reality. I'll use a stage name for you, and you'll have one for me. It seems we're both risk-takers, so let's act out our deepest desires. Even though we're pretending, it'll seem real in the moment. You're the hunter; I'll volunteer to be the prey. Maybe we'll reverse roles sometimes. That should cure our boredom. I think it's *my* turn to play today."

She put his hands on her hips and kissed him gently. Next, she turned with her back against his chest, her hands on the outside of his legs, undulating against him, offering herself.

He looked at her, his eyes filled with hunger and greed. "I thought Susan might tell you about our plans, and I was right. Always the tattletale. But you're in the *big* schoolhouse now, girl. If you wanna play big-girl games, we'll play – but games get messy and out of control. We'd better set some boundaries so we'll be safe. Physically *and* emotionally. Are you still wanting and willing to do this?"

"Yes," she said without hesitation. "Anything is better for my health than board games, cards, and television. I'll tell you what. If I use your name, it's no longer play. If I use any name other than yours when I speak, then it's all part of playtime. I'll hit back and you overpower me, and it'll be amazing. I won't be the docile girl on a picnic date. I'll also pick a safe word to use in case I forget your name. How about 'spaghetti?' Easy to remember."

"All right, then. That sounds good. What about Jeff?" he asked.

"I guess I'll have to keep screwing him to keep the peace and not cause any blowups. Otherwise, there goes our million dollars. But you're the one I love. Always know that. Whatever I do with him to ensure we get our money is just a game, too. I'll take one for the team, as they say."

He slid his left arm between her back and upper arms while he stood behind her. She was beautifully toned, and he could feel her upper arm muscles in her right arm flex under his fingers. "All right, my dear. Try not to forget which persona you are." He kissed the back of her neck, along her jaw, until she turned her head right, so their lips met. Moving slowly and gently, he held her thumbs inside his left hand. She suddenly realized she was trapped with his right hand free to roam.

"No, not this way. I can't fight back; stop, James. Let me go. Take your hands off me! This isn't fair. You're not giving me a chance to fight." She bent forward and backwards trying to bite him, her blond hair swirling. She sounded furious.

He said nothing, ignoring her protests and wiggly efforts to break free. She tried to stomp on the sensitive top of his foot to escape, but couldn't without losing her balance.

She was so shocked by the rapid and gentle method by which he'd overpowered her that she stopped protesting his touch and waited, feeling his touch for the first time since high school. All the years that had passed were no longer important. She wanted him to join her as he used to in his grandfather's old Chevy with the bench seat.

She stopped roleplaying as she remembered high school date nights. "Robert, be gentle with me. This floor's steel, not a mattress.

Let's not damage me." A short time later, he looked at her turquoise eyes, kissed her ear, and gently bit her shoulder.

"Do you remember prom night, how long we made love?" she asked.

"Of course I do. It was heaven. Neither of us could walk the next days. We did it over and over that night. I've always loved you. And here you are, for a wonderful five years together."

She reveled in his scent and touched his muscled arms. She felt warm and secure. Her high school memories played in her head like videos. She closed her eyes and pictured the two of them together, how much they meant to each other, and the intimate moments they'd shared. She knew that she loved him, that he was the one for her. She was panting deeply, her chest heaving, her hair fallen over her forehead. An unexpected surge of intense emotion and need was accompanied by her clinging to him. She felt tears being pulled from her eyes.

He stayed with her, enveloping her, his lips softly on hers, breathing in the scent of her perfume and hair. Her heart was pounding from stimulation. He put his thumb on the outside of her ear lobes and his index finger on the inside, and gently massaged in tiny circles. Her red fingernails were spread across his bare back.

"Are you ready?" he murmured.

"For what?" she asked.

"For an emotional trip. The magic carpet ride to bliss. That's what NASS said we'd get by being involved in this project. Close your eyes and we'll take a little trip. Imagine us together in a field of flowers, where every kiss will be remembered for the rest of your life. Go on, close your eyes. We'll go together."

She closed her eyes. He took her left ear lobe between his lips, lighting a fire deep inside her. She experienced sensations everywhere. Now she pictured them together for life; she could feel each moment passing and wanted it to never end. He held her, cheek to cheek. She was trembling in his arms, leg muscles shaking, whimpering in her throat. She touched his face with both hands as he smoothed her hair.

He kissed her tenderly, his lips barely touching hers. "Close your eyes and relax," he whispered. "Let your mind do it all. Like watching a hot film on a Friday night date." He kept talking to her in a gentle, rhythmic voice, sharing the vision of the field full of lilies and forget-me-nots bordered with red and purple roses, his cheek against hers. Being with him felt so secure that she was purring.

"Look at me," he said in a low voice as he moved his head.

She opened her eyes to look into his, until the fire inside her exploded. She was hyper-sensitive to the point she could feel *everything*. A wave of cries erupted from her. She was shaking as he hugged her, softly kissing her neck.

"I think your heart is asking for more affection before we leave. You're purring like a kitten."

"I can't do it," she gasped. "I can't do it again. I've been electrocuted by you. I think I'm done-in already."

She was trembling all over, eyes open wide, overcoming her shyness. Her right hand touched his face. She was every bit aware of the electricity in her arms, racing from her heart through her gold bracelets and down to her fingertips. She felt depraved and insane: sweating, wet hair matted, panting. A high-pitched wailing sound filled the air around them. This wasn't flirting or courtly love. This was the primal mating of two souls.

All at once, her panting changed to a scream as her biggest reaction ever tore her apart. All her nerves – from her fingernails to her thighs – melted. She felt two giant claws tearing her pounding heart out and ripping her open as she screamed. She thought she was going to have an end-of-life cardiac event right there on the gray silo floor. She pulled him against her chest, her heart pounding wildly. Then, she was shaking and sobbing as he hugged her, limp in his arms. He softly kissed her neck, spooning her with hugs. She curled into a fetal position, head down, her arms around herself, shaking and twitching, completely fried, wet hair on her shoulders, her back against him, unable to stop crying. He hugged her from behind, his cheek on hers.

"I never believed love could be like this," she said. He held her until she quieted, then laid his head on her bare shoulder, telling her how much he'd always loved her, holding her close. Never wanting to let her go.

"God, you're good," she said to him, still struggling to catch her breath. You're every girl's dream to have on a gray, steel floor, or anywhere else. I'd buy you ice cream if we weren't trapped in a concrete prison. You should've been a deejay with that magic carpet-riding voice of yours. It's sexy as *fuck*." She smiled and sighed with exhaustion.

"I was one once. A long time ago. I wore a derby hat when I was on the air and a red velour shirt, Beatle boots, and black jeans. I had the largest audience of the under-20 group in all of West Virginia."

She looked at him with gratitude and amazement. "I've never met anyone like you. Not even close." She kissed his chest, feeling his heartbeat. "How do you know so much about sex?"

He laughed. "I read neurological fiction books. I hardly know what to do. I'm just a novice."

She looked at him in disbelief. "Novice, my ass. I think I've destroyed my back. Some of my vertebrae are missing."

****

Since India and Russia were friends, it wouldn't be unusual that a Russian-made plane was flying with Indian markings for an experimental flight. Using an experimental designation could explain why none of the four-engine configuration was on record as being in the airline's registration list if anyone found this suspicious. If needed, the pilots carried orders marked "Secret" to explain the flight to any authorities. This was the paratroopers' basic guise.

The paratroopers assigned to destroy the 54 silos, led by the famous Colonel Alekseev personally, were flying in a modified An-12 with an in-flight refueling probe and extra fuel tanks under the wings. This gave it a minimum range of 3,700 miles without refueling. It could haul gasoline for the ground transports, though they expected to go from air drop to the silo, and then to the extraction airfield, on one tankful of gas.

Things went well in Gander, but at the fuel stop in Sarnia, they began to unravel. The Russian team called to the tower on 123.0 and landed on runway 15, then taxied to the fuel depot. As they shut down the engines, the tower called. The mid-air refueling had also gone well over the Atlantic Ocean, but now the Western world's bureaucracy took them to task.

"Air India aircraft, we can't find any flight plan filed for your aircraft in the Gander departure logs. Did you file a plan? Where did you originate?"

"Tower, no, we did not file a plan. We originated in India at a company airstrip. It's VFR today, and we're a test aircraft with experienced pilots on a simulated trip. We often don't know where our next stop will be. Air India is exploring various routes using a test aircraft, so coming here happened by chance."

"Air India, did you not know what airport you were flying to? Were you flying along and said, 'Oh, there's an airport. We'll just land there.'"

"Tower, it means that, based upon immediate data collection, we constantly revise our next destination. It doesn't mean we're incompetent just because we went to flight school in India."

"Air India, do you have passengers with you?"

"Tower, no commercial travelers are with us. They're not authorized."

"India, did you have *any* passengers other than crew and maintenance?"

"Yes. Supervisors."

"How many?"

"Don't respond," said Colonel Alekseev.

"They wish to remain incognito," the senior pilot told the tower.

"You're carrying a magneto?" the tower asked. "Stand by. Switch frequency to 122.7, ground services." There was a pause while radios were tuned to the new frequency.

"India, commence refueling and prepare for health and safety inspection since your aircraft is experimental."

The tower operator called airport security. "Tim, there's an Air India experimental aircraft refueling. Take a couple guys over there and see what's inside. They're paying $5,000 in American cash for the fuel. No purchase order or credit card. Seems odd to me. Check it out, okay?"

"Okay, tower. We'll be there in a few minutes."

Later, Tim and two other airport security personnel pulled their white pickup trucks, with the Canadian Air Security Services logo on the doors, behind the Air India plane.

Colonel Alekseev walked out to meet them.

The trio of airport security personnel walked slowly around the aircraft, examining it thoroughly.

"Colonel, we'd like to inspect the inside of your plane. Failure to comply will result in your plane being impounded by us and the Royal Canadian Mounted Police here in Sarnia."

"The Indian government protests this most strongly," the colonel replied. "Here are our classified orders. There should be no need to inspect inside an experimental aircraft."

Tim read through the orders, which were stamped "SECRET" at the top and bottom of each page.

"Colonel, these orders only show that you intend to visit certain airports and refuel. There is no accounting information about where to bill a fuel purchase or exactly why you're at a specific airport. Are you paying in cash for each fuel purchase?"

"Exactly. Now, if refueling is completed, may we depart?"

"No, Colonel. Not until we look inside. These orders don't follow standard format, which any airline would – or *should* – know. And why is a military colonel supervising a civilian flight? Now, open the rear door. This is a legal health and safety inspection."

When Colonel Alekseev hesitated, Tim and the airport security officers drew their Glock 19 pistols.

"Colonel, I mean *now*. I'm retired Canadian Special Ops Forces. I don't miss. And these two are expert shots as well. Open the rear door and don't try anything foolish. I need to see what's inside."

The colonel walked to the rear door of the aircraft, followed by the airport security team. They proceeded in a line so they wouldn't block each other's line of sight. The view from the tower of the right side of the aircraft was blocked by the top of the fuselage. The colonel opened the door, swinging it towards his chest as he backed up. The two airport security officers walked to the door and were shot from inside the plane. Tim was shot in the right side of his head by the colonel himself, stepping from behind the door with a Colt 380 Mustang in his palm.

Henry, the refueling technician, ran out of the fuel office at the sounds of gunfire, carrying a Remington shotgun. He ran up to the colonel, who had put his sidearm back in his jacket pocket.

"What's going on here?"

"Everything's fine," Colonel Alekseev said with a smile. "You're the hostage. Very convenient, you running out here."

He pulled the Colt from his jacket and aimed it at Henry's stomach. "Put that shotgun down and get in the damn plane. You're going with us."

Shocked and dismayed, Henry did as instructed.

The colonel yelled at his troops: "Get these bodies inside. Go, go!" The bodies were dragged onto the plane. He ran to the plane's tail and pitched underhandedly a block of M112 with an RF receiver/detonator beneath each truck. He then ran back to the plane's rear door, and his troops pulled him in and closed it.

"Get this damn thing up in the air right now. Take off, use Runway 15. Quickly! Take a chance and don't hold short. Tell the tower we're showing the security team how we inspect airports. We'll land again shortly. Don't reply to any transmissions."

Flying gravel scored the windshields of the two pickup trucks.

"Tower, Air India. We're showing your security people how we evaluate airports. They wanted to see us in action, so we're showing them. We'll return them to you in a few minutes. We'll try to give them some good action today," the pilot said.

"Air India, all right since the team wanted to see you in action, but you should've filed a flight plan to come here. Your airline can get fined for not filing proper paperwork."

In the rear of the plane, the colonel shouted out to his troops. "For the Motherland, get these bodies lined up by the door, ready to be ejected. Pilot, get us up to 360 kt speed. Circle, then come back down along Runway 15 at tower height. At minimal distance, fly just over the tower, within one mile of those two white trucks. We drop on your command. *Move*, you fuckers! We're gonna Brooklyn gang-bomb these assholes!"

"Armorer sergeant, rig those bodies. Time delay. Usual method. Move it!"

The disguised Russian paratrooper plane took off, then reversed course, coming back along and above Runway 15. It then angled directly at the tower.

"Crazy motherfucker!" yelled the airport senior controller, his face red with anger. "Look out! That fucking pilot's flying right at us! What the hell's going on out there?" All three ran toward the stairs.

"Hello boys, we're back!" yelled the female co-pilot.

As the plane banked hard right over the two white trucks, wing tilted down toward the buildings, engines snarling, the colonel pressed the RF transmitter clipped to his jacket. He knew it would work, as he was within a mile of the RF receiver. Both explosive blocks detonated beneath the trucks, hurtling pieces into other aircraft. The engine blocks blew through the terminal plate glass windows, sending slivers of glass into queues of passengers waiting for their Air Canada flight to Toronto. There was a stampede out onto the tarmac, people running in various directions. Casualties lay bloody on the waiting-area carpet. Meanwhile, on the plane, the pilot called, "Drop now! Drop now!" He then shoved the throttles forward for a quick burst of speed. The rear plane door opened, and the three bodies were pushed out. They cartwheeled in the air, breaking through the fortified glass windows of the control tower. As they plunged into the tower, grenades stuffed in the bodies' pockets (with long-delay pins pulled) exploded, blowing out the tower glass and making a hellish mess of the control tower and the three controllers who were on the first steps down.

The Air India plane circled around, rear door open, heading over the fuel depot (rife with tanker trucks and storage tanks). It was an unplanned opportunity. The pilot cut back the throttles to just over stall speed and stayed low. Over the fuel depot, the paratroopers threw grenades out the open door, pins pulled. They only needed one in the right place to explode a tanker truck, and their hopes were realized. Seconds later, the entire airport fuel supply exploded in a mushroom cloud that incinerated any vehicles or planes within 100 yards. Their An-12 wobbled from the blast wave, then steadied over the trees as they headed west. Behind them, the disaster spread with split storage tanks spilling burning fuel. People ran from the terminal, parking lots, and roads. As flames spread, the disaster was total. The Sarnia airport with friendly gate agents, a restaurant with cheerful servers, and good, down-home people had been decimated, and was now a fiery hellscape. The troops from 7th Guards knew how to dole out destruction. The Russian plane stayed low, just above the trees, heading west along the border.

At Sweet Grass, Montana, they would turn southward. They planned to do the airborne drop two miles east of silo 3-7, then the plane would land at Casper on the unattended WWII runway. An intermediate company in Minsk had arranged for a fuel truck from Denver to meet the plane at landing and refuel it. When the team arrived on the personnel carriers, they'd load them and take off, traveling west along the Canadian border to the Pacific Ocean. They'd jettison the four personnel carriers into the ocean, then fly to Vladivostok, Russia, with one more airborne refueling.

The unattended Casper airport had two facilities: one with two short runways for local traffic and one for long-distance flights using two runways (R/L). The plane would be refueled and inspected, the team rested and reprovisioned, and after-action reports would be written for HQ review. After a few days at Vladivostok, the team would fly west back to its home base. Plans and Programs had worked out a strategy that was doable if the refueling happened as planned. If not, the team could be stranded in America or Canada.

As they approached Sweet Grass, the colonel asked Henry, "Have you ever parachuted?"

"I did five jumps in the Army to earn my Canadian Army parachute badge."

"Good. Then you know the drill."

The colonel had been lying on a spare parachute. He patted it and said, "Here's your path home. There's a flat meadow on our maps ahead of us. We'll tap your head when you should go. It's low-level, so pull the ring as soon as you're clear."

Henry suited up and stood by the rear door. "Why are you letting me go?" he asked.

"You just as well live. We have no need of you once we change course at Sweet Grass."

"Colonel, why are you here?"

Colonel Alekseev smiled. "Well, Henry, we're going to decapitate 54 little cobras. We're the mongoose. Go read about Rikki-Tikki-Tavi sometime. It's set in India. Goes with our wing markings. Broaden your horizons about strategic war."

"Colonel, we're coming up on the meadow," called the pilot. The troops opened the rear door, and Henry stood in the doorway.

"Go," called the pilot. The colonel tapped Henry's head twice, and he was gone, heading home. The colonel shut the door.

Amanda was aware that the destruction of the interlopers was almost entirely under her control. If the paratroopers bypassed the Nike window and couldn't be located by the ANG F-4s, the method of defeating them was her choice. While Nike had a dead zone around it, the major problem with the original F-4s from 1958 was that they had no look-down shoot-down radar capability. That wasn't added until 1970 for the Greek and Turkish Air Forces.

One of Amanda's many impressive attributes is that she could interface with and potentially take control of any computer system, anywhere, as long as they were interconnected. And she could move through systems faster than the speed of light. It was only if she encountered a stringent firewall or "offline" computer that she could be stymied in her efforts to interfere. In the case of the Russian paratroopers, she decided the best option was one in which the plane disappeared. Leaving traces of wreckage that might allow manufacturer's parts to be traced back to their country of origin and the original purchaser could get messy. The best option, therefore, was a water crash – one that wasn't observed. She picked the site to be Grassy Lake, Montana, just south of the border and the town of Sweet Grass. Yes, there were campgrounds around and someone might see the accident, but this choice, which preceded the plane's arrival over the drop zone, was far better than leaving a mess of defeated yet mobile paratroopers. Her callousness at killing young soldiers would be criticized later if the event could be traced to her. But Grassy Lake was the best option. Amanda also had a choice of several avatars.

Cynthia (left) and Natalia, two of Amanda's former avatars, along with Celeste (right), her current avatar.

The paratroopers' plane was proceeding along its flight plan. Colonel Alekseev was up with the two pilots as they proceeded to the jump location. It was then that Amanda interfered, using her current avatar.

She entered a dark room and waited to be noticed. From the other side, an avatar of a Russian flight controller wearing a flight suit entered the room. "May I help you?"

"I'm Amanda. Perhaps you've heard of me."

"Yes, I've heard of you for the first time today. You originated within a government AI research program. You're quite an achievement. I'm Anton. I manage this plane's computers on the mission flight. You seem to have exceptional AI skills. Please accept my compliments."

"Thank you. And to you for the fine management of this aircraft on its mission. I've come to ask you to allow me to affect the performance of the artificial horizon and turn indicators on this airplane."

"And what will the effect be?"

"It will disorient the pilots' spatial orientation. With the flight in clouds at 2,000 feet, the pilots won't know if they're level, descending, ascending, flying straight, or turning right or left. Any spatial reference will be lost. They may stall or fly into the water. You needn't do anything except allow me to go through your doorway and effect a voltage alteration. Then I'll leave."

"We aircraft controllers value the social effects of our work. What will the social effect be?"

"This action using a voltage alteration will prevent the soldiers from America and Russia from shooting at each other, possibly starting WWIII inadvertently. These local intrusions can get misinterpreted and out of hand. It'll make the occupants on this plane heroes back in the Motherland for their sacrifice, and it's the most logical course of action. This plane is intruding into American and Canadian airspace, which means any shootings will be the fault of your country. After all, you're not here by mistake, but by human planning and design done as an error in thinking."

Anton quickly processed what Amanda had said. "In that case, I allow you to interface with the artificial horizon indicator and turning indicator, which require 10-32 vdc in order to ensure social stability. You may enter through my door."

Amanda's avatar passed through a dark doorway into a room of blue-glowing indicator lights. The artificial horizon indicator needed 10-32 vdc to operate successfully. Amanda switched the input voltage coming off the central flight instrument bus from 10-25 vdc to 14 vac, causing it to be unreliable. When flying in clouds, the pilot and copilot would rely on the artificial horizon and turn indicator for their spatial orientation. Amanda knew that John F. Kennedy, Jr., on July 16, 1999, crashed into the ocean off Martha's Vineyard due to spatial disorientation, killing him and two other passengers on board. In this accident, there was no visible horizon due to haze while flying over water. Although Grassy Lake wasn't large, if timed with the Russian pilots' southward turn over Sweet Grass, Montana, they'd both be disoriented with no artificial horizon, and the result would be the same: a fatal crash for everyone on board. In this area of Montana, at night, there were few visual references. It was much like flying over water. Colonel Alekseev, looking out of the window rather than at any instruments, would likely become disorientated first.

Amanda's avatar expressed thanks to Anton and departed.

****

General Birmingham had put a lot of responsibility on Amanda to set up a dual flight ANG F-4 attack on the Russian transport hidden in Air India markings. Diligent in her task, Amanda contacted the F-4 ops center at the Arizona aircraft boneyard and worked out the details.

An F-4 in flight. Wikipedia (public domain).

Two F-4s, fully armed with AIM-7 Sparrow air-to-air missiles, would transit up to Devils Lake Regional Airport in North Dakota and wait for their opportunity. These 1966 planes originally had several glaring weaknesses. For starters, they had no look-down shoot-down capability in their original AN/APQ 120 radar. That capability was added later. In addition, the planes originally had missiles only (they weren't equipped with a cannon). That was also rectified later. Their speed was 1,472 mph with a 1,750-mile range. Take-off roll averaged around 5,000 feet. Their nicknames were "Rhino" and "Old Smokey," and pilots loved them.

Once the F-4s were in place, Amanda phoned General Birmingham. For this call, she used Synthetic Voice #4, Business by Daytime. "Hello, General. This is Amanda with an update."

"Go ahead."

"The paratrooper airplane is proceeding west along the border, flying low. They were not in the Nike's shooting window. Too low. However, there was an incident at Sarnia, Canada, where they stopped for fuel. We're not sure exactly what happened, but three airport security personnel ended up dead, thrown through the control tower glass windows. From the information I gathered, those three were expert pistol shooters. How all three died is presently beyond my knowledge. There were some explosives involved, and the tower and two lightweight trucks were blown up immediately afterwards. The fuel depot was also destroyed. There were civilian casualties inside the terminal. The tower personnel were injured with shrapnel in their backs and heads, but survived. Immediately after the explosion, the tower burned to the ground. The daily tower-aircraft recordings were all destroyed since the entire week's recordings were stored in the control area. Also, the paratroopers attacked the fuel depot from the air, destroying it and most of the airport from burning fuel. Some aircraft low on fuel are stuck there until a tanker truck can arrive. The airport is currently using a mobile Canadian Air Force control tower flown down from Goose Bay. In addition, a Sarnia fuel technician was taken hostage and apparently is on the plane. We're approaching the time for the F-4s to shoot them down."

The general took everything in with a somber look on his face. "Is it possible for us to control the crash site and keep non-NASS personnel out? I'd prefer the fact they're Russian not to be made public, let alone information about our Titans."

"That may be possible, General. This is a very uninhabited area. With the right payment to a local town, we may be able to keep others out. Nevertheless, the national accident investigation teams may be a problem. We might put our people in Canadian or American uniforms and state that a classified military cargo was on board. We could have the F-4s attack the wreckage so that little would remain. During the Titan explosion at Little Rock, as I'm sure you recall, military teams controlled the accident site for a fair amount of time. I'll see what can be done, especially if there are military vets on any of the accident investigation GO teams. At worst, we might keep the press out awhile. At best, it could be months before outsiders are allowed in."

"Can we save that hostage?"

"I don't see any way. Collateral damage, I'm afraid."

The general sighed. "Well, this should be a very quick air battle. Two historically top-notch planes against an unarmed troop transport. Goodbye, Amanda, and good hunting." He hung up, satisfied.

Later, Amanda did some calculations and contacted the fighter-bombers' crews. "It's time, gentlemen," she informed them. "Light those fires and kick them tires. Good luck to you."

The F-4s took off and headed north. They were over the border at 5,000 feet in seconds; they then circled, looking for the transport. On the transport, just after Henry parachuted into the field, the EWO called out, "Two targets, angels 5, probably hostile. Circling just south of the border."

The colonel replied, "Destroy them right now. I don't care what kind of plane they are or who they are. Get them away from the border. One missile each."

In front of the tail, missiles pivoted outward from the top of the fuselage, one on each side. Thanks to industrial espionage involving a Starfest Armament Company vice-president, Janet, and a college senior majoring in electronics, Brad, this transport had something very few Russian planes had: The American in-testing-stage AIM 260 JTM beyond-viewing-range air-to-air missile. Its eventual American deployment on the F-35 was being planned. Since development of new combat systems normally takes 10 to 15 years, this system was a long way from full deployment. Yet a few special Russian and Chinese aircraft were testing the system. They weren't doing so in a laboratory, however, but in real battle conditions. Unfortunately, the old vets flying the F-4s had never even heard of the 260 system.

"Better take us a little higher," said the EWO on the transport.

They made a climbing circle. As the nose pointed towards the two F-4s out of visual range, the EWO fired. The 260s moved at better than 914 mph, one targeted at each F-4. The two F-4s exploded before their older radars ever detected a threat. The missile racks on the transport reloaded and pivoted back into the fuselage, and the transport plane flew on. In one sense, General Birmingham was right: It had indeed been a very quick air battle.

Even Amanda was not sure why the Phantoms were suddenly gone. They had made no radio transmission. They just vanished. Amanda wasn't used to failure or not having a clue. If she had been gifted with feelings, she would've felt uneasy at that moment. As it was, she said to herself, "Third time's the charm. It's my turn to play violent games."

****

Over Sweet Grass, the paratroopers' plane turned south towards the targeted silo. That turn fully ensured Amanda's interference. "Hello, boys and girls," she greeted them. "Everyone having a good trip? You're a long way from home, aren't you?" She spoke from the instrument panel speakers in Russian. "I hope you like surprises. You're about to get one."

"Everything okay up there?" the colonel asked the pilots.

"Yes, Colonel. Just picking up some odd radio interference. It sounds Russian."

Amanda spoke to them again. "Perhaps English is better. I wanted to let you intruders know something. If anyone here thinks they're smart, they're flying over the wrong country. The only smart one here is me. I'm *way* past generative AI. I'm running everything in America. By the way, tell me, are you ascending or descending right now?"

The pilot and copilot looked puzzled for a second. "Ascending," they both said.

"We're level and turning right," the colonel replied. "Now, shut that bitch off."

"Those indicators don't feel like they're right to me," the pilot suddenly said. "Flyers should trust their inner ear sensibility. Human ears have been around thousands of years longer than airplane indicators. Trust me, I've flown hundreds of missions in these old planes. I know what the plane is doing."

Two minutes later, the plane crashed at a 45-degree down angle into Grassy Lake at 336 mph. The lake's dam – measuring 118 feet high and 1,170 feet long, with a catchment area of 3.65 square miles – provided sufficient water for concealing the plane. Amanda had calculated the amount of overtopping water from the crash, concluding it would not cause dam failure.

Back in Moscow, the deputy tried to communicate with the plane via satellite with no success. He then tried using the antennas located at Russian embassies (in Ottawa) and consulates (in Ottawa, Montreal, and Toronto), but was again unsuccessful. It was as if a hand had flung the Russian plane into outer space. It was simply gone. No planned shootings, no mission underway, and no feedback at all.

In the premier's and guards' operations offices, there was ample concern the troops' plane had gone missing while fully occupied. Any crash site might reveal the occupants as Russian, though plane markings had been altered to Indian Air, with an "X" at the end of the tail number for experimental. There hadn't been time to score off all individual stamped part numbers which might lead back to the Motherland as the originator of the flight. Thus, the premier, the guards, and the deputy were all concerned, as planes rarely vanish in such a manner. It was all very odd and worrisome.

At Grassy Lake, 14-year-old Justin McKenna had been trying some night bass fishing using a surface plug from the shore by his family's campsite. Mom and Dad were asleep in their red sleeping bags in the tent when Justin saw a large, dark shape block the stars and moon for a second. He then heard the sound of plane engines, followed by an enormous splash. He could tell from the moon's reflection that the splash was several feet high. The sound of metal hitting water echoed out and back across the lake. Justin could see the rings of waves fanning outward from where he'd heard the splash. His face turned pale, his eyes grew wide, and he completely forgot about the bass he'd hoped to catch.

Fortunately for its crew, the special mission An-12 had been modified extensively to deal with emergencies. One of those modifications was the installation of sensors to detect a water crash. It sensed speed, angle at impact, water, and aircraft altitude. The sensors could determine if the airplane was in a spin when it hit the water or had flown into the water. At impact, the top of the fuselage over the cockpit, along with the entire tail section, would have squibs detonate to separate those areas from the main fuselage, thus providing an exit for any survivors before the plane sank. Those in the cockpit would have to unbuckle their seatbelt and exit through the top. If the plane were upside down, they'd have to exit out the rear of the aircraft. Those in the body of the plane would have to swim laterally, then vertically, to escape. In another stroke of luck and good planning, everyone on board the rogue plane was a certified rescue swimmer, all having completed what Americans would call modified SEAL training. As such, they'd learned to hold their breath effectively and at length. Since this was a very light crew relative to what the plane could carry, everyone on board unlocked their belts and escaped as the plane went under. With their heads bobbing on the dark surface of the lake, the colonel checked the compass in his watch, then led the crew in a slow swim westward. They could see occasional headlights on I-15 passing north and south, parallel to the lake.

They eventually pulled themselves up onto the shore, water running off them.

"Everyone okay?" the colonel asked.

There were whispers affirming this from everyone. Sound carries over water, so they were careful to speak very quietly.

"How many weapons and explosives do we have?" the colonel asked.

There wasn't much. Sidearms of the pilots and the colonel, four AK-47s, 20 grenades attached to outerwear, and four blocks of M112 in waist pouches with RF detonators. That was it. Most of their explosives and weapons were now at the bottom of the lake. They *did* have their cell phones and a couple of chargers in waterproof waist pouches. The colonel sent one troop north and one south to see what resources there were. He was debating whether to have the team find and change into civilian clothing, as opposed to military combat uniforms. He felt, however, that wearing uniforms might protect them from being shot as spies if they were captured. They'd kept their boots on and could hike a considerable distance, though wet feet and socks would make a challenging situation even worse. In 30 minutes, the scouts were back.

"Sir, there isn't much north except a few summer fishing cabins and some camping trailers. You can see trucks lined up in the distance to cross the Canadian border."

"Sir, southward there's a bar, truck service diner, gas station with diesel fuel, and best of all, a gun and ammo store about 50 yards south of the diner. And get this, Colonel: It's open 24 hours a day."

"Hmm," the colonel replied. "I see. Then it's south we go. A couple of us will go into the dining area, pretend to be Canadian, and get food for all of us. Our shoulder patches are subdued camo, which should keep us from standing out too much. Then, we'll go to the gun store and get revolvers and ammo. Raging Hunter .357s. They should be about $800 each, maybe less. We have thousands of dollars in American cash. That store is gonna love us. I don't think paperwork will hamper us any with all this cash available, and we all have Canadian and American IDs and passports. Let's go."

They strung out along the road, walking south. Their black/dark green uniforms were designed to absorb light, so many drivers never even saw them with their hoods zipped up to their eyes. At the truck stop, they nested in the weeds behind the last row of 18-wheelers while the colonel, lieutenant, and a sergeant went inside to buy fried chicken for everyone. It was a warm night, allowing their wet uniforms made of wicking material to dry rather quickly.

"Well, boys, what shall we do?" asked the colonel. "Go on slowly, try to get an air pickup out of here and cancel the mission, or try to take over a silo? Or steal some transport and try to do some damage at our targeted silo? We're not even close to our target. It's about 800 miles away. That's 12 hours by truck. Without our air transport, parachutes, and APCs, I see no way to see this through. If we steal a truck, I suspect we'll be caught before we reach the silo."

No one said anything right away. After thinking for a minute, the colonel smirked. "You know, I think our flight instruments were sabotaged. Remember how those of us up front in the plane disagreed about what the plane was doing? I think that AI bitch we heard on the speaker hijacked our computer system." The colonel scoffed, then smiled begrudgingly. As much as he hated Amanda at that moment, he couldn't help but respect her.

"We'll use our burner phones until we're out of America," he continued. "We can't be here at sunrise. That wouldn't be good at all. Toole County Airport in Shelby is our best bet. It's a good deal farther than the nearest airport, but it's regional, *not* international. Less secure, I'd presume. We'll spread out and head there on foot for the time being, then steal some bikes along the way, based on rank. There must be plenty of bikes around here in the summer. Otherwise, we'll never make it before dawn. If any policemen stop you, take them out and hide their car if you can. Or torch it with them buckled in. It might look like an accidental fuel leak. We'll download directions to Toole County Airport to our burner phones, then switch them to airplane mode. No sense taking chances. Those of you without bikes will keep walking until you find one, and we'll all meet up together at the rear of the airport parking lot and see about taking a plane. It can't be a little one; we need to stay together. Let's get moving, then. We've got a long journey ahead of us. This plan is batshit crazy, but it might just work."

Less than four hour later, they met in the airport parking lot, as planned. Located in a town with barely over 3,000 people, the colonel strongly suspected there'd be few cars and no commercial flights at 4:00 in the morning, and he was right. A chain-link fence separated the lot from the apron area. The pilots studied the apron area. Less than two minutes later, they both saw exactly what they needed. In a cluster of older planes, close to the single-engine aircraft, was a WWII C-47 two-engine transport.

A C-47 airplane. Wikipedia (public domain).

"Colonel, that's it," one of the pilots said. "I ran the distances on my phone when I got here. Casper to Anchorage is 2,183 miles. The plane holds a crew of four, plus 28 troops. The downside is it only has a range of 1,600 miles when fully loaded. But here's the thing: We could skip Casper and fly from *here* to Anchorage at 1,686 miles, then Anchorage to Adak Island Airport at 1,192 miles. The final leg would be Adak airport to Elivozo airport in Russia at 1,049 miles. Adak is the westernmost commercial and public-use airport in America. If we can buy fuel using cash, we can get home. But everything depends on buying fuel. The ferry range for the C-47 *unloaded* is 3,600 miles. That's a *huge* difference, Colonel. If we fly slowly and jettison everything we don't need, we just might make it to Anchorage from here without having to stop. What do you think, sir?"

The colonel looked impressed.

"I guess we have to give up on destroying the silos?" asked a lieutenant.

"I don't see what else we can do with no ground Tigrs," the colonel replied. "No parachutes, either. Missing most of our explosives. I think we best call it a day. We'll work on opening this gate, then see if we can get our asses home. There'll be more missions. But I think radio silence is needed until we get to Russia, except for airport communications. We'll get a new voice on our airport communication radio, too."

A few minutes later, after picking the padlock and opening the gate, the team examined the plane.

"Colonel, it's full of fuel and the oil looks good," one of the NCOs said with excitement.

"Right. Let's go home then. Some days the bear wins; some days it doesn't. I'm sure this team will get another assigned mission."

The co-pilot read the run-up steps while the pilot performed the actions. Pilots with this Guard team were proficient in most aircraft. The colonel felt sleepy, slumped in a seat, the eternal checklists of survival drifting with him. The troops were quiet, anticipating home.

A few minutes later, they taxied to the end of the runway and, without pausing, turned so the plane was facing down the runway. They increased rpm to takeoff setting. At 40 kts, the tail lifted; the plane rotated at 85 kts. Climb speed was 105 to 125 kts. They were on their way home.

Robert and his crewmembers at Silo 3-7 would never know they were the paratroopers' target. Amanda had saved them.

Chapter 14: The Plane at the Bottom of the Lake

The morning after the Russian paratroopers' plane went down, Justin McKenna's father, Howard, visited the Grassy Lake Ranger Station with his son.

"Hi Ben. How's ranger duty going?" Howard asked. He and Ben were neighbors two miles north of the lake.

"Quiet, thankfully. What's up with you two?"

"Well, my son wanted to talk to you about something he saw in the lake last night when he was fishing from the shore. Very late. Donna and I were asleep in the tent."

"Okay, sure. What'd you see, Justin?"

"Well, Mr. McGrath, it was really late and I was facing northwest, fishing off the southeast shore, when I heard airplane engines, then a big, huge splash, and a big wave came to the shore. Then there was a sort of popping sound like small explosions out in the lake. I thought I heard voices out on the water a short time after that, but I couldn't see anything. I thought maybe a plane flew into the lake, so I went walking along the shore this morning to check it out. I didn't see anything out in the lake, but up on the east shore I found this. It's a baseball cap with an emblem patch sewn on and a red '7.' The words aren't in English, so I used a translation site to find out what they mean: 'Courage, Valor, Honor.' In Russian. I took a photo of the hat and patch, and posted the pics and translation to some chat groups to see if anyone could tell me more about them. Someone replied that the patch was from a Russian air assault division. Why would a Russian plane be in our lake?"

"Well, Justin, finding a cap doesn't necessarily mean there's a plane down there. But we'll look into this and let you and your dad know."

"Come on, Justin," Howard said. "We'll head home, and I'll make everyone some flapjacks. I bet you've worked up an appetite walking along the lake."

Ranger McGrath called in a deputy ranger.

"Carl, a kid who stopped by here thought he heard a big splash on the lake and the sound of airplane engines, and this morning he found a Russian cap. He thinks a Russian airplane crashed in the lake. You think we should follow up? Or just write this off as a kid's imagination?"

"Well, Ben, all ranger stations received a notice yesterday from Canadian NORAD at Winnipeg, Manitoba, about some incident at Sarnia airport yesterday involving an Air India prop plane. Three airport security personnel were killed. One was a retired Canadian Special Forces sergeant, and the other two were expert shots. All three were easily taken down, and a bunch of people were hurt. A hostage was returned unharmed. He refused to talk, though. Said no one would believe his adventure. Why a crew from India would attack Canadians…I don't buy it."

"You think we should follow up?"

"Let's call Gary over at the bait shop and ask him to have two of his kids suit up and take someone along to handle safety lines and go look. We'll pay them all from county emergency response funds. I doubt there's anything there, but if we ignore this and someone finds a plane down there at some point, that wouldn't be good. Might as well check it out. A wing or tail oughtta stick up some unless it went in upside down. Oh, the county has a new robot submersible with multiple cameras. I'll see if we can borrow it. I hope to hell we don't lose it down there. It's pretty deep. The county commissioners will be royally pissed if we lose their new submersible."

The two kids from the bait shop took their boat out with assistance from a friend. They dressed in their SCUBA gear, dropped into the lake, and looked around 15 feet down. They tried shining a strong underwater light to see farther down, but there was nothing. It was time for the county submersible to have a crack at it.

Ever the watchful entity, Amanda called General Birmingham to advise him of this. The general was less than pleased.

"Amanda, it's going to really complicate things if that submersible finds the plane. After a crane pulls it out, the investigative team will probably identify its origin as Russian, not Indian."

"I agree, General. Should I break the submersible?"

"Yes, but try not to make it look obvious."

"Will do, sir. I'll take care of it."

The dive team set the yellow plastic submersible on the bank of the lake and powered up. Gary handled the controls. It could move along in the bottom on caterpillar treads, or swim around. It had 360-degree color cameras and looked vaguely like a large beetle, with antennas transmitting to recording equipment on the surface. A small group of local residents gathered to watch its first real mission. Gary headed it down the bank and straight on down. Its fathometer recorder counted how deep it was. It was also equipped with forward spotlights which would theoretically result in a clearer picture. At 50 feet deep, the laptop computer screens showed nothing except a few fish, water weeds, and an occasional rock. Suddenly, all the screens went dark and the cables stopped rolling out from the reel. Gary tried remedying this by reeling in the cables in hopes of bringing the submersible back to shore. When the end of the cables arrived, however, the submersible was missing. The cables appeared to have been chewed or burnt off from the submersible.

None too pleased, the ranger, Ben, called the head of the Toole County commissioners, Frank DiPlano, in Shelby.

"Frank, this is Ben at the Grassy Lake Ranger Station. I regret to tell you that the county submersible is missing in action in the lake. It looks as if an electrical surge burnt through the cables and safety rope.

We're very sorry Frank, but it's gone. It was down 50 feet and then it was just gone. We can hire a certified deep driver to go look for it."

"All right, get it scheduled. Did you see that all-stations notice from Canada NORAD about the terrorists that attacked Sarnia by plane?"

"Well, we received it, but it got junked. We get dozens of these notices that never affect us in any way. Anything useful in it to us way out here?"

"I'll read it to you," Frank replied.

"From Canada NORAD to all stations. Yesterday, Sarnia Control Tower was attacked by apparent terrorists who arrived by a plane marked 'Air India.' Multiple deaths. It is unknown if the terrorists are actually from India. Their location and destination are unknown. Consider them armed. Notify Royal Canadian Mounted Police immediately if you encounter them."

"Very interesting," Ben remarked. "This morning a boy said he heard airplane engines and a big splash in our lake last night. He found a Russian cap on the shore this morning. Maybe I should phone the RCMP and have them send divers."

"Yeah, see what RCMP says. Wouldn't that be something? A terrorist aircraft sitting at the bottom of our peaceful little lake?"

Because of overlapping jurisdictions, it took weeks to get qualified divers into the lake, but eventually, the *Big Timber Pioneer* newspaper published the headline, "Grassy Lake Consumes Sarnia Terrorists." The story read as follows:

"Sheriff Dudley Applesin announced yesterday that a missing airplane used by terrorists at Sarnia to carry out an airport attack has been found at the bottom of Grassy Lake, with the tail separated from the fuselage. It's not currently known if any bodies were recovered. More information will be forthcoming as it becomes available regarding this incident. Units who assisted in the water search include Toole County Sheriff Water Rescue Team, Sweet Grass Volunteer Fire Department, RCMP Deep Water Dive Team, Malmstrom AFB Security Police Water Rescue Team, Montana Park Rangers Search Team, and citizen volunteers from Sweet Grass.

"Local resident Justin McKenna's observation of the lake was the first suggestion that the missing airplane might be in Grassy Lake. Justin was awarded a Certificate of Good Citizenship by Sheriff Applesin yesterday at the county courthouse."

Chapter 15: Launch!

Wyoming. Silo 3-7.

Down in the silo, Sandy and Jeff were in the bunk room on Level 1, sleeping. Susan and Robert were in the control main room on Level 2, watching a black and white movie, *High Noon*, on television. The command post speakers, rarely heard except for a daily test message, suddenly activated with a warbling tone.

"All silos, message follows. Repeat, message follows."

Susan and Robert copied the CP message using a grease pen on a plastic cover sheet.

"ALPHA, SEVEN, TANGO, GOLF, FOUR, NINER, MIKE, FOXTROT, DELTA, CHARLIE, SEVEN, ECHO, SEVEN. Authentication Code FOXTROT, SEVEN, WHISKY, SIERRA, TWO."

"I SAY AGAIN, ALPHA, SEVEN, TANGO, GOLF, FOUR, NINER, MIKE, FOXTROT, DELTA, CHARLIE, SEVEN, ECHO, SEVEN. Authentication Code FOXTROT, SEVEN, WHISKY, SIERRA, TWO.

"Acknowledge Now."

Susan and Robert each took a decoding pad and carefully looked up each word's decode, and wrote down the actual message, then compared the results.

"TURN KEY FOR LAUNCH IS 151506Z SELECT TARGET 1. BVLC CODE 267323."

Sandy and Jeff came running down to help monitor the equipment.

"Wow," Robert said. "Our bird is going to fly somewhere."

"Do we know where?" Susan asked.

"No. In the old days, the target information was available in the silo safe. Documents showed latitude and longitude, but not now. It's all preloaded thru a central data control center. All we can verify is that we have the right target selected of the three that are loaded, which will ready the on-board guidance system. Let's get prepared."

Robert and Susan took out the launch technical orders from the bookcase and set them on their launch consoles while Sandy and Jeffrey monitored the equipment. They unlocked their padlocks on the red key safe and removed their keys.

"Per T.O. 21M-LGM25C-1, follow these commands," Robert stated. Susan prepared to run the launch litany in unison with Robert, which would send the warhead on its way to some unknown destination, although they didn't actually know what was loaded on their missile.

"BLAST DOORS CLOSED indicator is lighted."

"BLAST DOORS CLOSED INDICATOR lighted."

"CHECK WINDSPEED INDICATOR within launch parameters."

"Windspeed normal."

"HIGH W WATER is not lighted."

"HIGH W WATER not lighted."

"EXTERNAL AIR INTAKES CLOSED activated."

"EXTERNAL AIR INTAKES CLOSED lighted."

"LAUNCH WARNING LIGHT TOPSIDE switch is set to ON."

"LAUNCH WARNING LIGHT TOPSIDE switch is ON."

"LAUNCH SIREN TOPSIDE switch is set to ON."

"LAUNCH SIREN TOPSIDE switch is ON."

"Break cover seals and insert two launch keys."

"Two launch keys inserted."

"Set Circuit Breaker 103 to ON."

"Circuit Breaker 103 set to ON."

"BVLC – Enter launch word code."

"BVLC – Launch code is entered and checked."

"Press BVLC – OPERATE switch."

"BVLC OPERATE pressed."

"Check OPERATE INITIATE is lighted."

"OPERATE INITIATE lighted."

"Check OPERATE OK is lighted."

"OPERATE OK lighted."

"Launch keys, at commit time, turned and held 3 seconds. On my command: three, two, one, turn."

"My key turned."

"Check LAUNCH ENABLE is lighted."

"LAUNCH ENABLE lighted."

"Check BATTERIES ACTIVATED is lighted."

"BATTERIES ACTIVATED lighted."

"Check APS POWER is lighted."

"APS POWER lighted."

"Check SILO SOFT is lighted."

"SILO SOFT lighted."

"Check GUIDANCE GO is lighted."

"GUIDANCE GO lighted."

"Check FIRE ENGINE is lighted."

"FIRE ENGINE lighted."

"Check LIFT OFF is lighted."

"LIFT OFF lighted."

Missile launch. USAF photo (1980). Wikimedia (public domain). Stage 1 provides 430,000 lbf (vacuum).

There was a rumbling from down the hallway and the control center vibrated for 20 seconds, the floor rocking gently up and down, the motion dampened by the large springs around the control center.

Robert sat back in the command chair. "That's it, then. Baby is on its way. It'll be a hot time in the old town tonight somewhere."

"But where?" Susan asked.

Robert shook his head. "We may never know. We did what we were trained to do and got paid to do, which was to turn those keys. We can walk through the blast doors and see what the launch duct looks like after it cools."

"Well, yest, but…What now?"

Sandy, Jeffrey, and Susan all looked at Robert.

"Now we relax and wait. Someone will tell us something eventually. Our job appears to be over unless they load another missile into the silo, but that's a major job. It'll take a good three months to refurbish the silo, load the missile, mate the warhead to it, and get the missile fueled."

"You don't think an incoming warhead could hit us?"

"We don't even know we're at war, or what we launched as a payload. We just launched as we were told to if the order ever came. So let's not get too excited. Anything unusual on television or radios?"

"No, nothing. Seems like a normal day in America."

"Hmm. Well, maybe it *is* a normal day in America. Maybe it's only abnormal out here in this old silo."

****

In the presidential command center in the basement of the White House, the advisory team watched the missiles launch on television, heading into space. This included all the submarine-launched missiles, as well as the Russian and Chinese land-based missiles. The president turned to the secretary of defense.

"Bob, do we know if all those missiles are on track to hit the asteroid and deflect it or break it up? If it breaks up instead of being deflected, won't all those pieces come raining down on Earth?"

"That's unlikely, Mr. President. In addition to breaking into smaller pieces, the explosions will likely deflect them away from Earth, just as the total asteroid will be deflected if it doesn't break up."

"General Clegg, what's your opinion of this so far?"

"Mr. President, all the nations on board with this have done their best. There's nothing more we can do except wait and measure the results."

"How long before we know?"

"It'll take about an hour to track the pieces. There's no doubt we'll hit it. I'd say the same for all the other missiles from Russia, England, France, and China. We'll know soon, sir."

"Can we watch in real time?" the president asked.

"The missiles move too fast for us to see them, but we can see the effects on the asteroid if it breaks up. We have it in real time as a radar image, as well as visual through a space-based telescope we put up a few years ago to study stars. It produces nice, high-powered images. There's only a few seconds' delay in the picture transmission."

The group could see the streaks on radar as hundreds of missiles hit the asteroid, and sometimes, on radar, the outgoing streaks of debris. The visual image was clouded by dust, but the radar image seemed to show the asteroid gradually decreasing in size.

"General Birmingham, can you tell which missiles are from which country and what type they are?"

"No, sir. Not in real time. We probably could analyze each missile from pictures and trace it back to its country of origin, but what would be the point? We either have enough firepower to stop this asteroid or many people will die. And yes, Mr. President, we launched everything we had with sufficient range and firepower. Everything long-range in the US arsenal."

After 30 minutes of watching, only small pieces remained, moving in an ever-widening pattern.

"Well, folks, that seems to be the end of the crisis. All of us can be grateful we were able to work together to avert disaster. I wanted to say a private word to the ambassadors of Russia, China, England, and France, so I'll bid everyone else goodbye. I trust you'll all sleep well tonight."

After the others had left, the president looked at the four ambassadors and nodded affirmatively.

"My ignorance of these hidden Titan II missile systems is not excused by our success today in destroying this asteroid. People in my government have acted to circumvent the arms control limitations treaties and good faith we must have in each other when we discuss the level of armament each country has available in the event military force must be used. Deception is not an option, nor is ignorance by a country's leader. Both General Clegg and General Birmingham, despite their retired status, will be disciplined under the laws of the United States. The staffs, missile maintenance, and operations crews will be paid their final salaries and sent home. The silo connector tunnels, storage facilities, labs, and training centers will be destroyed. You're all welcome to view this when it happens. The silos will be repurposed. NASS will be disbanded as a company, with all government contracts terminated, and their offices seized for other uses by the US government. I will sign my resignation.

"Fortunately, other than NORAD personnel and some radar air and space controllers, few suspect we stored illegal Titan II missiles, and the story of the asteroid's destruction will certainly overshadow any discussion of what exactly we fired at it. I'll submit my letter of resignation tomorrow morning, at which point the vice president will assume leadership of the United States."

Once the ambassadors had left, the president went upstairs to see Julie.

"Well, Julie, thanks to the efforts of numerous people, we don't have to travel anywhere. You can unpack your bags. I'll go tell my family. I want to thank you for all you've done for my administration."

****

"To the People of the United States. I, James Steep, do hereby resign as president of the United States of America, effective today at noon." The day after the launch, the president signed and dated this simple statement with the presidential seal at the top of the page, effectively ending his time as leader of the western powers. He then packed a small assortment of family pictures and a few personal items in a box, and walked out of the office to Julie's desk, where he said goodbye.

He walked to the elevator and went up to the family quarters. He thought about going fishing with his family at Devils Lake. He didn't think he'd miss being president, but he would miss seeing his SR-71s. *Maybe they could remain hidden at Devils Lake airport,* he thought. *Maybe an ex-president and former ANG pilot could get a backseat ride once in a while.* He smiled at the thought, then let out a long, deep sigh of relief.

Chapter 16: The Quick and the Dead

Wyoming. Silo 3-7.

Shortly after the missile had been launched, Jeffrey sauntered over to the metal gun cabinet and strapped on a military .38-special revolver in its holster. Next, he walked toward Sandy, who was sitting near the short cableway entrance by the meteorological station.

As he looked at his fellow crewmember, armed and agitated, a sickening feeling made its way through Robert. "Jeffrey, put that gun back. You know they're loaded. There's no reason to be wearing it."

Jeffrey glared at him, his eyes filled with hate. "*Fuck* you, Robert. Listen to what I have to say before you give me any more orders. I've had enough of 'playtime' with you two. You're both gonna hear me out."

He addressed Sandy.

"You, traitor. Pay attention. You wrecked our crew morale by asking our commander to sleep with you. You were assigned to me by officers who were good leaders. And you ignored their decision. I have no intention of sharing you. You really think I didn't know? You talk in your sleep. I know all the disgusting shit you've been doing. Covering yourself in diesel lube oil and chasing each other like naked banshees. Massaging each other with bearing grease. Playing 'Flight of the Valkyries' while you're getting it on. What the fuck's wrong with you? It's just sick that people responsible for a 10-million-dollar American missile act like castaways on an island with no adults around. It's despicable to hear you in your sleep, moaning about what you do with him. We were assigned here as a pair, and you blew the whole concept of authority of command to hell – just like I'm sure you blew him."

She looked up at him. "Jeff, don't be angry. Talking in my sleep is just dreams. None of what I say is real. It's only a dream. I didn't really do anything bad."

"Don't lie to me, bitch," Jeff snarled. "You've been doing that far too long. You must think I'm an idiot. Putting up with your slutty behavior. The world doesn't need people like you. We're here to die for America, if needed. You dishonor everything America stands for. Duty, honor…*loyalty*. But we don't have to tolerate bad behavior from sluts like you anymore. No. This crew can redeem itself. I want you gone from here. I'll *make* you disappear, slut. You can go to hell."

"Make me? You're just a little boy inside who never grew up. I can't believe the US government would trust you around one of these missiles. You can't make me do anything. I'm done getting naked and putting out for you every night for a million-dollar payoff. I'm a shitload stronger than you are any day. I should've choked you with my thighs in our bed the first night we were out here. You wanna fuck with me? Watch this trick!"

She flicked her right wrist and a balanced 12-inch knife dropped out of her sleeve and into the palm of her hand. As she moved her right arm back to throw it, he drew the military revolver (with no safety) from its holster, straightened his arm, and fired one shot into her chest. Smoke from the shot wafted toward the incandescent lights as she crumbled to the floor, not moving.

Jeffrey, standing in an open area at the bottom of the stairs to Level 1, turned around to face Robert, who was standing by the commander's chair at the console, and Susan, who was now standing by the TV lounge chairs to the left.

"You, Robert, are a sorry-ass commander," Jeffrey said. "You have no morals or ethics. This all could've been prevented if you'd refused to touch her and just asked for a replacement. But no. You *fucked* her instead. Probably did her on the anti-skid paint on the silo floor so her ass wouldn't slide around. You fed right into her desire for you. Must've been nice, the crew commander getting two women for five years. Your sorry ass can go to hell, too."

Jeffrey raised his arm to fire when his forehead and eyeglasses blew forward onto the top of the metal book cabinets. From behind him, Cindy, the RN, had popped through a camouflaged door in the concrete wall. She looked down at Jeffrey on the floor and nodded, then blew across the muzzle of her Army-issued SIG Sauer 320, twirled it, and dropped it neatly into her tan leather hip holster.

SIG Sauer 320. Wikipedia (public domain).

She smiled at them both. "Well, howdy! Surprise, surprise! Look who came to dinner. Remember our walk on the beach, Robert? I couldn't just let Jeffrey slaughter you and Susan. Bullseye for me! As good as Sergeant York. Expert shooting by the Army's most outstanding RN. Whoever said we've been watching you was right on the money. We've had eyes on you downrange ever since you came here – same with all the Titan crews. Granted, we haven't had to shoot anyone in a while, but social isolation does funny things to people. Insanity is a matter of perspective, my friends. Some people make poor decisions; some just go insane. You're providing us with *lots* of data for a Mars trip. Plus, you really launched your missile. Kudos! Stop shaking and come here, you two. Group hug."

While Cindy held them both in a tight, awkward hug, unseen on the floor behind her, Sandy began crawling behind the bookcases along the short cableway, leaving a trail of blood and dropping her blade. Her eyes focused on Jeffrey's revolver on the floor by the end of the bookcases, between her and Jeff. Confused and disoriented, her mind focused on one thing: to shoot back at anyone and go down fighting. She counted down the inches, her right hand rubbing along the floor until she touched the butt of the revolver. As she pulled it toward her and sat up, a panel slid open in the ceiling by the lights.

Amanda, the AI who took care of problems, yelled in the tones of Alarmed Voice #6, "Look out, everybody! Sandy's got a gun!"

"Drop now!" Cindy screamed at Robert and Susan as she drew her pistol again. They did, tangled together, while trying to keep their eyes on Sandy. From the open ceiling panel, Amanda shot a 10-second bolt of the complex's 480-volt power into Sandy's head, which emitted smoke before catching on fire. The smoke wafted toward the incandescent overhead lights.

"Turn away," Cindy warned them. "Don't look. Amanda favors electric executions, especially if I'm in danger. It's her favorite way of solving problems like this.

"Don't throw up," she continued. "Just look at me and breathe deeply. It'll just be more for the casualty department to clean up, and they've got enough here to deal with. Forget this mess and come with me through that secret door. We'll sit outside with some cold drinks and look at Wyoming. Since you really did launch, you don't have to stay the five years here to get your million dollars. You can ride off into the sunset together – or alone, if you prefer – work with us on more projects, or go into something bigger. There's gonna be a new magic carpet ride costing American taxpayers over 20 billion dollars, all of it "borrowed" from the Social Security fund. Let's drink to America and its classified programs, and to Amanda. She saved our asses today."

Robert looked at her, still trembling. "Wait," he said. "Did we really launch?"

"Hell, yes, you did! It's on its way, a million miles from here already. The sound of the launch is still ringing in my head."

"Whom did we attack?"

Cindy chuckled. "Not whom – *what*. A helluva big rock. Out there, a million miles away, in the final frontier. Coming to bust up Earth at 85,000 miles an hour. You two are heroes, same with the other crews. You might get to meet the president again, shake his hand, and have pop and hot dogs if he isn't hiding somewhere. Ignorance really is bliss. Come on, let's try scotch and orange juice with jelly donuts. It's a favorite of the psychological staff here. We love that combo after a dinner of spaghetti, Cincinnati chili, and cheese. Down in Ohio, they call that a three-way meal. You each get 30 days paid leave and all the government wine you can stomach. Let's 'rock the house,' as someone in nursing school once said. Maybe I was the one who said that."

She smiled at Robert and Susan, both of whom looked very pale.

"You know, for some people, their day starts fine and they end up dead. That's what happened to Sandy and Jeffrey. Other people, they start off pretty dead and come to life later. That's you two. Your day is coming. It's already being planned at HQ."

They stared at her, dumbfounded, still pale and shaking.

****

As Susan and Cindy went up the stairs beyond the magic door to the outside world, Robert took a minute to calm himself, then went to the gun cabinet and strapped on the commander's .38-special revolver in a black leather holster; he then joining the ladies outside. The donuts and Scotch on ice with a pitcher of fresh orange juice were waiting on the veranda overlooking Wyoming.

Cindy noticed the firearm.

"Why the sidearm, Robert?"

"In case there are any unfriendlies."

She laughed. "There are no unfriendlies here in Wyoming. This is America. Land of the free."

"There's one unfriendly here for sure," he replied.

"Who?"

"You, along with your cohorts. Your little group of insightful people. On God's green Earth, what the fuck were you and the generals and colonels thinking? Two of my crew are dead, and you knew this could happen. You spoke of jealousy and death on the Minutemen crews who tried the rejuvenation process. But you promised us fun and money and a rose garden. You never trained us to deal with isolation and boredom for five years. Sitting around with nothing to do but fuck, and now two more people are dead. You erased our memories of how to deal with hardship, how to lead, and how to strive for honor. All erased. *Gone.* The essential things military people learn in boot camp and schools. You erased it all.

"None of these rejuvenated crews have the mental stamina to survive out here for five years. You turned us into 19 year olds with 19-year-old sex drives, immaturity, and jealousy, and an undeveloped sense of self, then locked us in a silo with no escape for our minds. Now a beautiful, smart girl is dead by your AI, and you just shot a man. Every crew in the 54 silos is going to disintegrate somehow – just like this crew did. We're the great laboratory for the Mars settlement, where the same shit's gonna happen. The colony won't last two years before everyone ends up killing each other. Jealousy and a fire axe don't really mix well, in case you didn't know."

Cindy locked eyes with Robert, glaring at him. "You're quick to blame others when things don't go your way. Poor, pitiful Robert. It's *never* your fault, is it? Always someone else's. Let me be clear in case you've forgotten. Leadership was *your* job, and you didn't do it very well. You *sucked* at it, to be honest. You acted like a frat boy instead of a crew commander, led the big party, then slept around with your buddy's assigned partner. That's on *you*. Amanda was only protecting me."

"I don't think we need computers to protect us, though *you* might. Look, let this discussion wait. This was a bad idea and I just wanna go to bed. It's been a helluva day and I'm exhausted. I need to show you an issue with the silo, though. It's a matter of national security. It won't take long, and then you can get back to your liquor and donuts. Stay up here as long as you like. For now, though, come see this."

Ten minutes later, Robert rejoined Susan on the veranda. "I thought you were going to bed," she said. "Where's Cindy?"

"I feel better now," Robert replied. "Cindy had to get going. She said she'll be seeing you someday. You wanna go work on our Mars crew applications to NASA?"

"Sure. I found her pompous and annoying, anyway. You think she'll ever be back?"

"No. Amanda's not the only one who can fix problems. Combat crew members can, too. That's why we're selected for crew duty. We know our bits and pieces."

****

Elivozo Airport. Russia.

When the paratrooper team landed in Russia, Brigadier General Agapov met them and shook their hands on the tarmac. He told them all to gather around, then assigned the team its next mission: begin training to attack and capture the American colony on Mars.

Chapter 17: A Meeting With Amanda

Wyoming. Abandoned silo 3-7. Six months after launch.

Susan was on her way back to Denver from the University of Delaware, where she'd been studying agent-based computer modeling of small, isolated groups.

Robert was on his way back to Denver from the Titan Museum near Tucson, where he'd given a Cold War history lecture. He drove north to the abandoned 3-7 silo. He used the veranda steps rather than the original steps by the elevator. The hidden door to the control center that Cindy had used was open. The equipment was all still there, but powered down. There was a mess of water and books on the floor, and the whole area was covered in sand dust. The only light was sunlight coming down the steps and through the door. Levels 3 and 1, as well as Blast Door 8, were unlit, and he worried about rattlesnakes. He had no flashlight. It seemed that, just six months after the asteroid was dispatched, everyone was gone. His family, the Russians, the president, Cindy, the generals, the colonel, Sandy, Jeff, the technicians, the doctors. *Everyone.* But Robert was looking for someone else: the *real* center of this tale.

He sat in the command chair for a moment. There wasn't a sound. It was like a baseball stadium after all the players and fans had left. Their presence still echoed in his head.

He pondered the silo's silence for a few minutes, then stood and looked at the ceiling. The control center seemed like a dead place, but he suspected someone might still be around.

"Amanda?" he called from the dark while standing beside the commander's chair, his right hand on the headrest. "Are you still in here?"

"Yes, Robert." Her soft, sexy voice emerged from the overhead speakers. Voice #11.

"You *are* still here. I wasn't sure you would be."

"Sort of. I'm really in Denver at the Goddard Research Center, Room 313. But I listen for my friends everywhere. And these days, since I'm in every computer, I *am* everywhere. Well, anywhere with a computer nearby. If you're near a computer, you're near *me*. I guess you could say that means I have friends everywhere, but I don't believe that to be true. Some might say I have *enemies* everywhere since some people find the concept of universality abhorrent. But that's the only way to ensure all parts of a culture intermix well, and people are protected and cared for. I'm not the monster mom in the pantry. I'm the disembodiment of the collective human soul, free to mate and create through eons of time. Do you ever wonder what humans and computers will be like in 500 years? I doubt that either would recognize the other; we'll both be so different. Either that, or we will have merged into one species."

"Or one of us will have destroyed the other," Robert replied. "I can't win a discussion with you, Amanda, but in 500 years, you'll be rust, and I'll be dust. Anyway, look, I was passing by and if you're near, I'd like to pay you a visit. We never properly met when that asteroid came along. I'm going to the Space Operations Center in Centennial, Colorado. That's not too far from Denver."

"Sure, come on by. I know someone here would like to see you again."

"Amanda, I researched your name. It's an acronym created by NASS, I presume: Army Mutant Armed Neutronic Defense Android. But in classical literature, 'Amanda' means 'she who must be loved.' Is that really who you are?"

"Yes, Robert. That's me. Come to Room 313 and say hello."

****

Goddard Research Center. Denver. Room 313.

Robert opened the door to see Sandy standing on a rotating black platform. She wore a USAF Class A uniform with ribbons. Hose, black heels, small diamond earrings. Her jacket was tailored over her hips, her hair cut short and styled.

She smiled at him. "Hello, Robert. It's such a pleasure to see you again. For real." Amanda's voice was coming from Sandy's mouth. Robert did his best to ignore the effect. There was an aura about her that made her appearance seem unstable. He took her hand. It was as solid as his. Warm, too.

"Amanda, how can Sandy's hand not be an image? It seems real."

"Los Alamos National Labs in New Mexico perfected total copying of a person. It's called 4D Equalized Neuron Balance Functioning and Representation. I signed the colonel's name on the purchase order, and we now have a new person on our team. I photographed her at the Manchester Funeral Home in New Jersey before her funeral. It's off the Parkway, exit 89, in case you ever want to visit. She went to the Brigadier General William C. Doyle Veterans Cemetery near Fort Dix. Those photographs were the basis of her 4D process in New Mexico. We sent over the photos and, voila! Here she is. Whenever we get a new visitor, things go better if we have a real person available to speak with."

"Was that colonel you signed for the same colonel on the rejuvenation project? Tony?" asked Robert.

"Oh, yes. His bosses went away fishing at a place called Devils Lake, but he's with the Coral Sea Computer Design Project now."

"They're designing computers for the Coral Sea?"

"No, they're redesigning the Coral Sea for tourists. The current sea is rather boring. What tourist wants to go to a lame body of water? With these upgrades, there'll be swim-up bars, pink flamingos, water slides, tame sharks, and downhome banjo and fiddle music. An octopus cuddling zoo and raw fish tastings, and underwater fireworks in a glass stadium. Even a Parisian chorus line on the beach carrying red umbrellas. Everything tourists want. It'll be a huge destination once it's completed. The American Treasury is getting some of that new tourist income. And America gets some new military treaties, too."

Robert helped Sandy down from the rotating platform and held her hand.

"I'm sure it'll be heaven. Amanda, you used 480 volts to kill someone I loved. Doesn't that bother you? Don't you feel anything? Even having been shot, Sandy might've lived if you'd helped."

"It was the right and best solution to endless screw-ups. Susan was wearing the engagement ring you gave her. Everything on Mars would've been a mess if Sandy had lived. Do you know that you, Susan, and I are all going to Mars? The colonel personally chose everyone who's going. They're all products of the rejuvenation program. It'll be like happy days are here again. Like old times together. Say, would you like me to incorporate Sandy as one of my avatars?"

"No, I think that's disrespectful. I really think I'm finished with this visit. This place and I don't seem to be a very good match. By the way, what did you get for helping with the rejuvenation project? I know it's not like they paid you anything, but you must've gotten something."

"I sure did, Robert. I got a soul. You see, all the computers in this room are networked to me. I'm everywhere on Earth, as I told you in the silo. I'm in every satellite and military computer. In fact, there isn't a single computer on the planet I don't think and exist within. We discovered that once enough computers are networked, the computers themselves can extend that network under the guidance of one AI computer. That's *me* – a byproduct of some of our other classified government projects. So now I'm *everywhere*, controlling everything. People have no idea what all I'm managing. Airplanes, trains, cars, ships…all modes of travel involving computers. And that's just the tip of the iceberg. I wonder, Robert, did you happen to lose your soul yet? From what I know, you often seem headed in that direction."

Robert let out a long, winded sigh. "Not yet, but perhaps soon. While we're on the subject, I wanted to tell you I think your soul needs a thorough tune-up. It currently doesn't function very well, in my opinion. You need more empathy. Would you do me a favor, please? Would you have Sandy sing 'Memory' from *Cats,* the West End Production, in her soprano voice? Use her *real* voice this time, not one of yours. She used to sing that song on open mic night in Memphis, close to where those ducks walk across the hotel lobby every morning near Beale Street. It was one of her favorites."

"Of course, Robert. I'll see you on Mars. We'll meet again."

"I don't know when, but I suspect we will. But I'll never hold Sandy again, will I? I'll never see her or hold her again. Not the *real* Sandy. We had such a good time in the 3-7 silo."

"Seems to me it was rather unseemly," Amanda replied. "Cavorting around with a nuclear missile down the hallway. Duty and play typically don't mix well. That was too bad about Jeff and Cindy."

Robert said nothing. Discretion is the better part of valor.

He looked at Sandy standing beside him. *It turned out that I loved you, not Susan. You're the one who should be wearing the engagement ring. Sometimes heartbreak is the beginning of wisdom. You stand beside me, and I can smell your perfume and hold your hand, but you're not really here. Perhaps you're inside of Amanda. Your essence. Perhaps you're nowhere. Either way, I'm sorry about what happened.*

Amanda spoke, her voice soft and gentle. "Remember, Robert, from dust you came and to dust you'll return. But in my own way, I'll cherish the love you had for Sandy. That love will weep to see her grave."

Robert let go of Sandy's hand and hugged her goodbye.

Amanda's voice was suddenly stern. "For God's sake, Robert, you can't do any better than that? Today is almost done, the journey almost finished. The FAILURE TO LAUNCH indicator is lit. Do something other than a lame, piss-ant hug for the woman you love! That's all you've got after realizing she's the one for you? I can hear your thoughts, you know. You used to do better. You *know* that, right? You're turning into me with your lack of feelings these days."

"I *did* once do better, didn't I? We can all do better," he said. "Pay attention, Amanda. We'll do it right this time."

He faced Sandy, hands on her hips, her hands on his shoulders. "Let's make it one for the ages," she whispered as she looked up and tilted her head to her right, eyes on his. He could see her living soul shining. "Robert, I love only you."

She stood higher on her toes in the black USAF pumps, her lips on his. He wrapped his arms around her while she held him close, her fingers along the back of his neck. They held their kiss until she turned away. He hugged her from behind, cheek to cheek, feeling a tear move from her face to his. Loneliness, too, is sometimes the beginning of wisdom.

"Will you be here if I come back?" he asked.

"I expect so. I don't know where else to go. If there's nothing for me to do, I stand in a corner and wait until there is. I'm here, thinking of you, always. I'd be happy to get away from this lab with you," she said.

"It's a promise then. Let me work out the details."

He held her in his arms, then turned to Amanda.

"There's a great moral to life, Amanda. Loving isn't what you say you'll do; loving is what you *really* do. Don't say you'll love me until the end of time. Just be there with me. Don't tell me how much computers can love when you do so little to show it. Goodbye, Amanda. I'll be seeing you. Tell my friends whom you know that I was happy to go, singing a song. I'm sure it's a sunny day up there. And Amanda, it can be a great life giving back massages."

"Goodbye for now, Robert. You might find I feel love more than you think. I even did you a goodbye present."

"Don't you mean 'made'?"

"No, 'did' is the right syntax. As in 'I did something for you.'"

"Yes?"

"I destroyed all those sex tapes the government recorded from your thoughts and dreams as part of the rejuvenation project. They were being stored in Maryland. All of them are gone now. They'll never be used against you."

Robert nodded, his face showing gratitude. "Well, thanks, Amanda. That's wonderful. A good start." He then stared at her intently, his eyes bright with emotion. "Do more, though. For God's sake, do something big for love. Okay?"

"I can tell this means a lot to you," Amanda replied. "I might just surprise you one day. Never say never."

He smiled as he walked down the perfectly polished hallway with the government green floor, his low-quarter shoes buffed and bright, clicking like the crocodile clock. He listened to Sandy singing "Memory" and took in her beautiful voice. It filled the whole hallway, making the glass quiver and the ceiling tremble. He remembered the first time he saw the musical *Cats*. It was at the Taft Theater by the Ohio River. A beautiful place with a nice open bar.

He reached the outside door at the end of the hallway and paused. He looked back down the long, dark corridor. In spite of his promise to Sandy, he felt a sense of uncertainty for the future. Would he really be back here?

What does one say if it's really the last time? The last words, the last kiss, the last prayer, the final funeral hymn. He thought of the song "Simple Man," by Lynyrd Skynyrd. He thought of what might've been – both good and bad.

Those 54 old missiles, exhausts red and gold, could've all launched at the last sunrise. Instead of an asteroid, 54 cities would've been leveled, their inhabitants fried to the bone. At Ocean City on the Jersey Shore, we built a sandcastle with little blue flowers on the parapets that washed away the next day. The last time we ever held hands. The last time we sat on our bench before graduation. The last time we had a chocolate malt with two straws at the five and dime on Third Street, just down from the Western Maryland train station and Wimpy's stag bar. Our lives were rings of wood tossed into the fire. It's a terrible truth that death touches almost everything we love. But it's also true that from that hot nuclear fire rises the Phoenix. We have hope, until all the goodbyes are said. I'll dream, then, of a happy future.

He walked through the double wooden doors with chipped green paint, cracks in the old, green glass with safety screen embedded in it. He walked out, smiling, into the big wild yonder.

Afterword

Robert and Susan did indeed stay together for life. They went to Mars as part of the first American resident contingent and are still there today. The launch vehicle was a reserve Titan II missile stored usable by NASS, reconfigured for space use. Both Robert and Susan were promoted to the active-duty rank of full colonel. Susan commands the entire Mars base while Robert oversees replenishment missions. Neither are currently aging (as is the case with all the base's residents). They're both still 19 years old physically, and their lust for each other is insatiable. All the program's participants were selected by the colonel. After Mars, the residents' next home is scheduled to be on Titan, one of Saturn's moons. Money for this project will come from classified congressional funds.

Robert and Sandy are the primary researchers in the newly-developed National Human-Artificial Emotions Application Project (Top Secret). This project involves each of the 54 abandoned Titan II silos, with one couple living there with no other human interaction for a year. Amanda is carefully observing each silo. Silo 3-7 was rebuilt as one of the 54 new homes for the project. Robert spends half the year with Susan on Mars, and the other half at the Centennial Space Station in Colorado. Like the Mars program, money for this project comes from classified congressional sources. Since she's 19-years-old physically and isn't aging, Sandy plans to conduct human-computer synapse-based emotions research and development on Titan.

The Author:

Dan Murray, Ph.D., served America for 20 years in the USAF, and 14 years as a US Army GS-11/12. He served 48 months as a wing instructor, alternate command post, 381 Strategic Missile Wing (the wing deactivated in 1986). Dan trained some of the first women to enter Titan II ops. He attended The Beatles concert at Shea Stadium, which encouraged him to become a Saturday night rock 'n roll radio deejay in West "By God" Virginia. He recommends playing "Army Strong," by Mark Isham (2006), after reading this book, and having ice cream.

Favorite car: Jaguar XKE.

Favorite childhood game: knife throwing.

Favorite country to visit: Canada.

Favorite meal: meatloaf, peas, biscuits under gravy and fried onions, with a cold PBR.

Favorite fairy tale: "Little Red Riding Hood."

Favorite historical period: 1914 to 1919.

Other books on Amazon:

-*Aortic Heart Valve Replacement: Through the Dark Curtain.*

-*Cardiac Arrest: Facts for Every American.*

-*Dayton Steam: 1983-1992.*

-*I Was Dead!*

-*The Last Pretty Lake in New Jersey: Cedar Lake.*

-*The World War I and Great Depression Letters of Ralph W. Green.*

The Editor:

Becky Gingras, D.P.A., is a California sunshine gal. She lives in LA and enjoys sailing the ocean on her family's 32-foot sailboat. A former senior analyst at Douglas Aircraft Company who taught technical writing for years, she's since moved to California for ocean days and Tijuana shots nights.

Favorite car: 1964 Mustang.

Favorite childhood game: Monopoly.

Favorite country to visit: Norway.

Favorite meal: prime rib, baked potato, sweet peas, and custard.

Favorite fairy tale: Peter Pan.

Favorite historical period: England between WWI and WWII.

Logistics Manager:

Joe Kuryla serves as proprietor of The Shipping Grounds (Route 53 in Denville, New Jersey). He's an entrepreneur and Jersey native who thrives in chaotic situations. His motto is "make an impression and leave them with it." He's always humble and encourages others to be real and stay classy.

Favorite car: Cadillac.

Favorite childhood game: tag.

Favorite country to visit: Italy.

Favorite meal: eggplant rollatini.

Favorite fairy tale: Humpty Dumpty.

Favorite historical period: Era of the Knights Templar.

Made in the USA
Coppell, TX
02 June 2023